I0827940

Bleeding Heart

bleeding heart

MELISSA GRAVES

ISBN 978-1-941530-01-6

Published by Interlude Press
http://interludepress.com

Book design by Lex Huffman
Cover Art by Buckeyegrrl Designs
Cover Art Photography ©Depositphotos.com/zhuzhu/nelka7812

THIS BOOK is dedicated to fandom, which has directed the course of my life in one way or another since I first connected to the Internet at the highly impressionable and hormonal age of thirteen, when all I wanted to know was where they kept the porn.

You inspired me to create, you encouraged me to share, and your love of what I have to offer has been one of the only consistent things in my life.

Thank you, from the bottom of my heart.

1

"It's the husband," Erica says, jabbing a finger at her iPad. "It's *always* the husband."

"Oh, come on," Brian replies, laughing at her insistence. "He's such a nice guy."

"That is exactly why it's him," she counters, tossing up a hand in frustration at his apparent inability to see what is so very obvious to her. "Besides, he slept with her sister."

"Before they were dating; that doesn't even count, and it doesn't make him a murderer. Geez."

"Lunch at the taco truck says it's the husband."

"I see your angle," Brian replies, smirking. "You've got a deal." He taps the iPad, pausing the television show they've been watching. "We should keep an eye on the door."

She brushes back her glossy black hair. Her almond-shaped eyes and petite frame show a weariness that matches his own. "It's been a long week. Besides, it's just past four-thirty; the rush is over."

Can't deny that, Brian thinks, *and thank goodness*. They'd had no less than six unidentifieds, and one volatile who'd done serious damage to the counter and the security doors before the police had arrived with their chemical spray and herded the poor guy off into custody.

Working the graveyard shift at a blood service center in downtown Chicago, Illinois is a job that could never be called boring. It's not that the vampires can't go out during the day—the fact that they can is one of the reasons they've been able to hide for as long as they have—but that they are stronger at night. They tend to handle their business and socializing between dusk and dawn and getting free blood at the center is often the first stop for many of them.

Coming on later in the evening means that Brian usually sees the more mature vampires—those who can wait, those who prefer to avoid the younger crowd that shows up as soon as the sun goes down. The downside to this is that he also sees, at times, the unpredictable ones—the ones who aren't regulars, the ones who wander in at all hours of the night. Between them, he and Erica have plenty of crazy stories to tell.

"I'm going to start tossing the expired blood," he announces, patting her on the shoulder.

"Bless you," she sighs. It's not a fun task, and they usually playfully bully each other when it comes to deciding whose turn it is, although she's his boss and could just assign the task to him.

Brian stops to use the bathroom and adjust his scrubs—the logo of a pair of elongated canines with one drop of blood hanging from the left tooth stands out in sharp relief against the starched paleness of the white shirt. His identification and security credentials, announcing him as a medical student and blood center employee, hang from the breast pocket. His thick, black hair has seen better days; his tanned skin is tinged with an unhealthy, pale hue; and his clear brown eyes are red-rimmed and tired. He can't bring himself to bother restyling his hair this late in his shift, or care too much about how exhausted he looks. Even though he has no one in particular to impress, he takes his appearance very seriously and would normally fuss with it no matter the hour. But Erica is right. It has been a hell of a week.

It always is, he supposes. They're only the second blood center to open in the city, and the program itself is barely five years young. There's still so little they know about vampires and even less that they know about how to serve them properly. On-the-job training can be wonderfully educational, but also unpredictable and sometimes overwhelming.

"Brian?" Erica sticks her head into the back room where they take their breaks. "Can you make sure that we get the AB neg front and center for the morning shift? I had one today. Don't go crazy, but at least two packets, just in case."

"Oh, wow, really? Okay." He keeps that in mind as he starts disposing of the expired packets and counting the fresh ones.

Three hours later, he and Erica walk each other to their cars. Per security protocols, after seeing each other out of the parking lot, they'll call each other when they are safely home and behind locked doors. Vampire-on-human violence is at an all-time low since the Outing, but it's not uncommon for blood center workers to become the target of hunger-related attacks, especially close to dawn.

Brian is half asleep by the time he gets home, Erica's voice a soothing hum over the phone as he shrugs out of his scrubs and falls face-first into bed. He usually spends these last few moments before he falls asleep contemplating how working the night shift has destroyed his social life.

Thank goodness for Erica, whose boyfriend and parents have gone out of their way to make Brian feel like part of the family. Erica works full-time at the center (she graduated last year), so everyone in her life is used to the schedule; whereas Brian is doing the summer program for experience, money and school credits while he works toward a degree in porphyrical (vampire) medicine. And his only local family, his older brother Michael, is a vampire and a lawyer who rarely has time for him.

"Mom's making your favorite today," she says.

"Same time as always?"

"Yep."

"I'll be there. You're awesome. Mom's awesome."

She laughs. "Goodnight."

"'Night, Erica."

He's asleep before he even ends the call.

Kyle is grateful for one thing at the moment, and that is that his life waited until the warmer weather set in to fall apart completely. It's not as if he has to worry about dying of exposure, but who the hell wants to run away in the middle of a freezing winter or a rainy spring? As it is, he's touch and go in terms of coping, covered in someone else's blood and stuffing a bag with his belongings while his aunt and uncle watch television downstairs.

They have no idea what's happened.

Truth be told, it's already beginning to fragment in his own mind, breaking down into a series of flashing images and sharp, high-pitched noises. The smell of sweat and fear and blood, always blood, forever blood. The muscle memory of struggle, grasping, tearing.

No one tells you that being a vampire doesn't actually make a damned bit of difference when it comes to self-hatred. Or doubt. Or fear. Or loneliness. It doesn't bring your parents back from the grave. It doesn't make the relatives who took you in out of obligation love you. It doesn't make you straight. It doesn't prepare you to deal with being psychologically tormented by your peers on a weekly basis. It doesn't prepare you for blacking out and waking up to a dead body and knowing—without knowing how you know—that you have killed someone, that at any moment you'll be discovered, and that this is it, it's over. Your entire pathetic life, such as it is, is over. It wasn't much of a life to begin with, but at least it was yours and maybe it might have been something, someday.

Murder is murder is murder, no matter that he'd been defending himself.

No one would believe that he'd allowed himself to be restrained and injured, not when he has such strength. No one would believe that Jeffrey had gotten hold of the chemical spray the cops use to temporarily weaken vampires and had used it on him. No one would believe it because while he'd killed Jeffrey he'd taken his blood; no one would believe it because he had come out of the fight physically unharmed. The injuries he had sustained had already healed; the bonds that had held him had been broken in the struggle.

His aunt and uncle wouldn't speak in his defense. They'd be embarrassed but happy to be rid of him, and they'd write him off as a bad egg, well disposed of, within the month.

Running is his only option now. He has enough money for bus fare and a couple of days on the road. That's as far as his plan can take him and, in a twisted way, he's almost thankful that he'll be able to accomplish that much.

He's a nineteen-year-old high school senior who looks the same as he has since he was sixteen and had been turned into a vampire: a boy of average height, on the slender side, with light reddish-brown hair, blue eyes and fair skin (the result of Irish genes, not vampirism). His powers are as juvenile as he is, his knowledge of vampire nature limited to whatever he has managed to gather from the Internet and school guidance counselors. No one had any sympathy for him when he was turned, and he sincerely doubts that they will now that he has human blood on his hands.

He stops for a moment before he leaves, taking in the sparseness of his tiny bedroom. It's frightening how little time it has taken to gather up the few things that matter to him. Frightening how little space these items take up in his bag.

Such a small life, crammed into an even smaller space.

He listens to the television playing downstairs. It's loud through the thin walls of his aunt and uncle's home. A laugh track plays, hinting at a sitcom. He wonders how long it will take them to realize that they hadn't seen him after the graduation ceremony.

At least he'd received his diploma. He laughs, and somewhere between gasps the laugh turns into a sob and he spends the last few moments he has gathering toiletries from the bathroom and crying like an idiot. He pauses to wash his face and hands clean; he'd love to wash off all of the blood, but he doesn't want to risk them hearing the shower, and besides, he simply doesn't have the time. He needs to get as far away as he can before morning.

The last thing he does before leaving the neighborhood is toss his vampire identification card in a garbage can several blocks from his house. The garbage will be picked up tomorrow and, with any luck, no one will ever find it. He has no idea what he'll do for blood while he travels (no card, no blood at the centers), but he's pushed it to a few dry days before and he can do it again if he has to.

Erica nudges Brian when the door opens. Security cameras give them full views of every inch of public space that vampires might occupy inside the center, but they make a habit of taking the extra step to communicate with each other when a particularly strung-out looking vampire comes in.

There's a shatter-resistant, reinforced glass wall between them and the clients. It isn't until this vampire is right up against the glass that Brian gets a good look at him.

Brian has seen vampires in every state from starving to over-fed, but he's never seen one look so completely lost before. The slender young man on the other side of the glass is not only underfed, but also exhausted. His hair is limp and there are dark circles under his eyes. He's clutching a coat around his torso as if it were armor, and his eyes glance blindly off the shapes around him. The fact that he's cold on a warm night like this speaks volumes. It doesn't require a medical student to tell that he's in bad shape.

Brian steps up to the microphone. "Hello," he says. "May I see your ID card, please?"

"I don't, um, I don't have one," comes the scratchy reply. Beyond a weariness in the tone, it's a lovely voice, delicate and youthful.

Brian nods. "Okay. Well, I can't give you a full serving as an unregistered individual, but I can give you an emergency ration, as long as you're willing to be tested for type and give me your information and a photo tonight."

Without testing the vampire for blood type and getting as much information as he can provide, Brian is not technically permitted to give him blood at all. They do have synthetic blood as a last-ditch offering, but that is not public knowledge—it's still in the experimental stages—and while it is Erica's call to give Brian permission to offer it or not, they've never done so unless a vampire was on the edge of losing consciousness then and there.

The young man's eyes go wild for a second and then instantly calm again. "Th-thank you, anyway, I—that's not possible."

He trembles and clutches his coat more tightly around himself. It's clear that the effort it takes for him to do this—to be polite and leave when he can probably smell the blood on the premises—is monumental.

"Wait," Brian calls.

Erica glances at him out of the corner of her eye. The vampire freezes halfway to the lobby and swings his tired eyes back to the glass partition. The ugly yellow light from the ceiling fixtures makes him look even sicker than he probably is. Brian turns off the microphone so he and Erica can speak privately. They're alone on duty and no other vampires are waiting for blood—it's almost six in the morning.

"I want to see him," he says. "He's not going to last much longer."

"Brian," she sighs. "We have to track their consumption. We have to be able to identify them if they're going to be on public assistance. We have to feed them the correct blood type. We can't just serve every vamp that walks in off the street. And you can't run him through all the red tape without an identity."

"We still have those portable testing supplies, right? The manual ones, not the ones connected to the network?" They'd gone digital shortly after the program had been established; the older testing supplies and recordkeeping systems had been retired before they had even had a chance to collect dust.

She stares at him, hard. "Yes, we do."

"And we have synthetic stores. I can do a quick test and give him something to keep him going. It doesn't even have to come from stock."

"What's got you so worked up over this kid? You've never—"

He blushes. "I just—don't want to see him collapse somewhere. He'll end up in jail, and you know what they do to unregistered vamps once they get them into the system." There is still so much prejudice against them—despite the fact that they don't deserve it, in Brian's opinion.

"All right," she replies, tapping a pen against the clipboard in her hands. "But only because it's almost the end of the shift and I'd really like to get home on time for a change. John's off today." She smiles, rolling her eyes at herself. "It's kind of crazy that we consider getting to sleep together for a few hours to be the best date ever."

Brian grins, squeezing her arm. "Not crazy. You're the best. We'll be in room two, okay?" He motions. "And you'll ditch the footage after?"

She brings the security camera for that room into sharper resolution with a few one-fingered taps. "After. But I'll be watching."

"Thanks." He turns the microphone back on. "Excuse me, sir? To your right there's a door. Go through it and have a seat in room number two. I'll be with you shortly."

The boy's whole form seems to shudder, but he goes. He probably thinks that he'll be asked to sit through an interrogation, only to be told that they can't help him.

Brian takes a deep breath and gathers the items he needs.

✷

The examination room is the size of a walk-in closet, with the same reinforced glass, counter and exchange drawer as the front room, only on a smaller scale. Its beige walls have seen better days.

"Could you remove your jacket, please?" Brian smiles. "I have to make sure that you're not concealing anything. Standard procedure—nothing personal, I promise."

The vampire quivers on his feet as he complies. Beneath his coat he wears drab clothing, muted colors in a bland style, nothing that speaks to personality. He's thin, but it's difficult to tell whether that's the result of hunger or nature; vampires don't show starvation the way humans do.

"Would you prefer to stand?" Brian asks. He hasn't collapsed into the chair on his side of the partition yet.

"Yes, please," he replies.

"Okay." Brian exhales. "I'd appreciate it if you would at least tell me your first name. Think of it as a gesture of good faith."

A faint laugh lights those pretty blue eyes for one heartbreaking moment. "I guess it doesn't matter in the long run." He wobbles on his feet. Brian wishes he would sit.

"Kyle. My name is Kyle."

"I'm Brian," he replies. "It's nice to meet you, Kyle. Thank you."

He sets the testing kit on the table. The synthetic blood packets are in his pocket. Kyle can probably smell them, but there's no reason to reveal them yet. He might react from survival instinct and Brian would rather it not come to that, more for the sake of Kyle's dignity than Brian's safety, which is more or less guaranteed by the glass.

"This machine will tell me which blood type is the best match for your nutritional needs," Brian explains. "We typically do a lot more testing at this stage for informational purposes, but we'll skip that for now, okay? I would really appreciate it if you would come back for that some other night, but for now let's just get you stable."

Kyle frowns. "Why are you making an exception for me?"

"I don't like seeing people suffer when I have the ability to help them," Brian says, letting his eyes meet Kyle's.

"Thank you," Kyle seems at a loss and shrinks in on himself.

Brian clears his throat. "I'll need a blood sample. Just put it back in the drawer and press the button when you're done."

The machine is like the blood glucose test used by diabetics: a spring-loaded device with a needle at the tip to prick the skin and an absorbent strip to take the blood sample. He explains this to Kyle. It's done quickly, and Brian plugs the strip into the machine and waits for results. This takes several minutes, as the machine is one of the older models.

"B positive," he announces, smiling. Nice and common—that's good. (Also, his own blood type, but he doesn't say that.) He reaches into his pocket and finds the correct packet.

Kyle's pupils triple in size in the span of a heartbeat, so fast that Brian actually pauses before releasing a breath he hadn't noticed taking in. Kyle frowns, closing his lips around the fangs that Brian knows are probably beginning to lengthen at the sight of the blood, synthetic though it may be.

He smiles reassuringly and passes the blood packet over by way of the drawer. "This is pretty self-explanatory. Synthetic, so you're not taking a donation away from us. And it's a full ration." He catches Kyle's wandering eye again. "But please—if you can. Come back. Let us help you, okay? You can eat here once a day, and I promise you that the real stuff tastes much better." He's trying for a smile with that last bit.

Kyle's cheeks darken. "I—"

"Not that I'd know, I mean, I've heard," Brian adds, feeling his face grow warm. Kyle is staring at him as if he's never seen a human like him before.

"Thank you, again," Kyle says, clutching the packet. "May I do this alone?"

Most vampires would rip into the packet without a moment's hesitation, starved or not. *How odd*, Brian thinks.

"Of course. You can leave when you're done. The doors will lock behind you."

When he's back on the employee side, Brian allows himself to lean against a wall and close his eyes. He's shaking and flustered and he isn't sure why, really. Something about Kyle, about their exchange, has rattled him.

After a few careful breaths, he forces it out of his mind. It's likely that he'll never see Kyle again, and there are thousands of vampires out there for him to worry about.

The synthetic blood tastes like crayons. In Kyle's current state, dirty and tired and alone and starving, this discovery actually makes him laugh until he cries.

Crayons.

He sucks the packet dry, and then, when he's on the verge of managing to throw it away, he rips it open and licks the plastic clean. It's not a happy moment for him, but then again he can't remember the last happy moment he's had; so he supposes this isn't saying much.

That isn't entirely true. That doctor was nice, he thinks, his chest aching.

After leaving the center he wanders, as he has been for the last five days. Five days in this city and he still has nowhere to stay. Surprise, surprise, homeless shelters—and everything like them—don't house vampires. The city doesn't yet have the funding to put in place security measures that will protect humans from their strength.

The synthetic blood may not have tasted good, but it improves the way he feels, at least physically. His muscles stop aching for the first time in days. He can see without blurry spots and walk without stopping every few minutes. His back straightens. It's not enough—he can already feel the hunger closing back in—but it's better than he's felt since he left home, and all it had cost him was his pride and first name.

He sits in the doorway of a shop to catch his breath. There's a vampire logo on the door, which isn't odd, really, the logos are everywhere now—in graffiti and to indicate blood centers and vampire-friendly businesses, and also on the news when vampire legislation is being discussed—but this one is different. It's got a drop of stylized blood coming from the right fang instead of the left and the color of the blood droplet is darker, closer to the real color of oxidized blood than the fire engine red of the official logo. He wonders what it signifies.

The sign above it reads "Mi Corazón Sangrante."

The words waver in front of his eyes. Now that he's sitting, standing up feels impossible. He curls up in the doorway, wraps his arms around his knees and slips into unconsciousness.

"He's about as appealing as fat-free cheese," are the next words Kyle hears.

A woman stands in the doorway where he passed out, staring down at him. All he can see of her is a pair of dangerously tall heels and brown ankles.

"I don't know," says the companion standing next to her. Kyle sees pale ankles, ballerina slippers. "He's kind of pretty under all that emo and street grime." Her voice is husky, like a smoker's.

Kyle tenses, his defenses falling into place. "Commentary is not necessary. I'm going."

"Wait," calls the woman who had compared him to cheese, stepping out onto the sidewalk. She's stunning: dark, long, wavy hair, coffee-brown skin, flashing eyes. She wears a slinky red dress that hugs her thick, curvy body from bosom to knee. "You over eighteen?"

"What—what does that have to do with anything?"

"Over eighteen?" she repeats, talking slowly, as if to a child. "New to the city? Only been a vamp a few years at most? Lost, alone, friendless? About to cry me a river? *Dios mio*, I am this close to falling asleep, you are that boring."

The second woman steps up next to the first and smiles. Her shoulder-length strawberry blonde hair bobs around her face. "What she means to ask is, do you need a place to crash?"

"Yes," he admits, because there is no hope of concealing this sorry state of affairs; but he shakes his head as he answers. "You don't know me. I don't know you."

"My girl here has a soft heart," the dark-haired woman says. "And let's be real, you're obviously out of other options or you wouldn't have passed out on our doorstep."

She's right. That doesn't make this a smart thing to do, but beggars can't be choosers.

"We have a bed, if you're interested. No strings attached," the blonde woman says.

He follows them inside.

Michael and Brian Preston have always had an up-and-down relationship—sibling rivalry, personality clashes, jealousy of each other's relationship with their parents (Michael had been close with their father, Brian with their mother), misunderstandings of each other's professional and life goals—the list goes on. Many of these issues have extended into adulthood without any sign of resolution, but if nothing else, they have learned to acknowledge one another. Michael has become easier to get along with and Brian has grown up a lot. He appreciates every tiny step forward, because one of his biggest fears once was that they would fail to address their differences and lose each other when they got older. He's especially grateful for this now, since Michael is one of only a handful of people who can understand what he's going through.

"You're thinking about him, aren't you?" his brother asks, spinning his tennis racket.

"I can't help it," Brian replies, shielding his eyes from the sun with his hand. "It's the ones I only see once that drive me crazy. Did they make it? Did they leave the city? Are they in the system, are they dead, are they just—forgotten? What if they had family?"

"I'd help you if I could, little brother, but we're not a hive mind," Michael replies sarcastically.

Brian smiles. "I know. I didn't—I don't talk about him with you because I think you hold the answers."

They take their places on the tennis court and begin exchanging volleys. Brian tries to lose himself in the exertion, but it's difficult; his mind keeps floating back to work, school and Kyle, in that order. After the second set, his brother calls a halt.

"I've got to get going," he says. "I'm meeting Jenn for lunch."

He slings an arm around Brian's shoulders as they walk to the changing rooms. Once there, he nudges him. "Hey. This isn't—I know that I've asked before, but I have to ask again. This isn't about Mom, is it? You latching on to these individual faces? I don't want you to get lost in a crusade. She wouldn't have wanted that for you, either."

Brian frowns. "No. I just want to help people, that's all."

"Thank god one of us gives a crap." Michael sighs in mock-relief and Brian laughs and hugs him around the waist. It's comforting to be held against his brother's taller, muscled frame, to see the affection in his brown eyes.

Today has been nice. They don't often make time for one another, and Michael hasn't been this affectionate with and interested in him for a long time. His genuine concern makes Brian think about his question in a way that he never has before.

The truth is, it isn't about their mother. Of course Brian had been devastated when they'd tried and failed to turn her into a vampire to save her from the cancer that was eating her alive. Scientific understanding of vampirism had been so lacking then; they couldn't have known that the experiment would not only fail to save her, it would end up killing her.

He keeps telling himself that she suffered less than she would have had the cancer taken its time to kill her naturally. Most of the time this fails to make him feel any better.

Since her passing, he has been consumed by a desire to make a difference in the field. He wants more than anything to provide the world at large with answers that might save people or, at the very least, help them to understand the vampires who share their world.

He has to try to make a difference. He doesn't know any other way to be.

*

The kitchen at the back of the club smells permanently of garlic, which Kyle finds ironic in a nod-to-nostalgia way.

His "sleeping the daylight away" turns into two days of swimming in and out of a slumber so deep that it feels more like a coma than anything else. Clara—the fairer-haired woman—wakes him up twice to feed him packets of blood. Real blood. It certainly does the trick. On the third day, Kyle wakes up and doesn't immediately feel the urge to go back to sleep.

Every night after that, they gather in the kitchen. The women speak Spanish interspersed with English phrases, smoke cigarettes, drink anticoagulant-laced blood from shot glasses and ignore him.

After about a week of this ritual, curiosity gets the best of him and he asks, "What are your names?"

"Elisa Martinez," the dark-haired woman answers, blowing a stream of smoke across the greasy table. "This is Clara Anders." She grinds her cigarette stub into an ashtray and tosses her hair back over her shoulders, motioning to her companion. "And you are?"

"Kyle."

Clara licks blood from the corner of her mouth and exchanges a look with Elisa. "Well, then. Aren't we all just chummy pals now?"

"I can't pay you for anything," Kyle says awkwardly into the silence. "I mean, the blood, the room, I—I spent all my money getting here."

"Let me guess," Elisa says, looking unimpressed, "you can't tell us where you came from or why you ran you away."

He frowns. "I appreciate you taking me in and feeding me, I really do, but if you're going to be rude in response to every damned thing I say, I can leave."

He doesn't intend to start his new life as he'd carried on in his old one, by allowing himself to be pushed around and talked down to.

She smiles viciously, pleased. "Kitty has claws. That's good." She lights another cigarette. "Let me bring you up to speed, *gato blanco.* The sign on the door, the reverse blood drop, means that this is an establishment where human folk come to get their suck on, safe and sound. They pay a handsome price for the service; sometimes in money, sometimes money and blood donations. It's legal and it's all consensual. It keeps us clothed and fed and everybody wins." She puffs, coughs, and goes on. "I have plenty of house rules, but I'm not going to waste my breath spitting them out unless you're interested in joining our little gang."

He stares at her as if she's just offered him a job plucking chickens.

She interprets this as haggling or ignorance, apparently, because she rolls her eyes in response to the look on his face. "All right, listen. I need a twink up in this joint. I'm bleeding—pardon the pun—gay dudes left right and center because I'm not selling what they're looking to buy. It's just a nibble, I want to be super clear about that, but when they pay for a nibble they want to cuddle up to a hot young male thing, *comprende*?"

"H-how do you know I'm—"

"Come the fuck on, kid," she sighs.

Okay. So he's never been what you'd call subtle in that department.

"What would I have to do?" he asks.

"Drink their blood. We'll teach you how it's done. In and out in fifteen minutes: They get happy, you get fed, and they leave cash. Some of our regulars donate, like I said, and the blood goes to the house or the blood centers if we get a surplus. We've got security guards. We've got a licensed phlebotomist—her name is Janice Pagle—on the premises during business hours. We donate to fucking charity so that maybe one day we'll all be able to sit in a circle holding hands singing 'Kumbaya' or some hippie shit like that. I let Clara handle the social justice end of our operation, can you tell? We own the building, so there's a room for you, just to sleep, of course—you'd have to share a bathroom and this kitchen. So what do you say?"

Kyle is overwhelmed.

That some humans enjoy the rush of being bitten and losing blood isn't a secret; it's a rather overdone trope in books and movies and on television. He'd just had no idea that they'd be willing to pay for it, or that the process could be so organized and clinical. He'd certainly never given a thought to the vampires who were paid to do the biting.

He can't help thinking about Jeffrey.

"I've only fed on a human once and it was a mistake," he replies, finally.

"He screams suburbia," Elisa says to Clara out of the corner of her mouth.

"So do half the babies who come through here," Clara replies, shrugging. "Look, we're not going to throw you into a locked room with a human, a napkin and a straw and bid you *bon appetit.* You'll sit in with another vamp until we're sure that you can pull it off solo. For now, you'll greet customers up front and help Janice with the donations. Legit business is a lot of work."

"And Mama needs a little vacay," Elisa adds, pointing to herself.

Parts of the offer freak him out and others seem too good to be true, but what it comes down to is that he has nowhere else to go and they all know it.

"I'd need fake papers," he says. "Fake everything. I can't use my old surname."

Kyle Hayes can't exist anymore, as least not as far as public record is concerned.

"Oh, baby," Elisa croons. "That ain't no thang."

"Welcome to My Bleeding Heart," Clara says, grinning and shaking his hand.

2

"You made it up," Erica says, swinging their linked arms as they walk to their cars. "You just don't want to share a shift with him."

Brian laughs and cringes at the same time as he reaches for his keys. "I'm not denying the truth of that second statement, but I really do have a seminar to attend."

"I love how you talk about seminars the way normal people talk about vacations."

"It's the first applied pharmacological conference porphyrical medicine, and I've been looking forward to it for weeks, and you can just quit judging me any time now."

"Oh, no, I'm with you there. It's going to be interesting." She stops suddenly between thoughts, her eyes settling on their cars. "Brian." She elbows him.

Kyle, the young vampire who stumbled into the center several weeks ago, is standing between their cars, his hands in his pockets.

"Kyle?" he blurts.

"Hello," Kyle replies, his tone friendly.

He's *okay*. All at once, Brian feels a tension he wasn't even aware of unravel inside his chest. A blush crawls up the back of his neck when he realizes that he's staring.

"You're looking much better," he says. "Um. I mean, you seem well. I'm so glad."

Kyle is wearing black dress slacks and a purple button-down shirt. He looks warm and comfortable in the temperate evening air. His hair is carefully styled into waves, and his skin is glowing white and healthy. He's smiling, the right side of his mouth turned up.

Brian exhales. He is gorgeous.

"Erica, could you...?"

"You're good?" she asks, under her breath. Technically, she isn't supposed to leave him alone with a vampire on blood center premises.

"We're good. No worries."

She nods and waves to them both. "Call me, okay?"

"Yep," Brian answers, his eyes on Kyle.

Except when they're blessedly, completely alone, he finds that he hasn't a single thing to say. His chest feels as if it's been wrapped in steel bands and his throat is closed. He's not sure why he's reacting this extremely; there's just something about Kyle that makes him want to either act out passionately or run and hide. Maybe one and then the other, because he's surely making an ass out of himself if any of these feelings are showing.

Kyle smiles, holding his hands up. "Unarmed. I'll take off my shirt if necessary, but if you're going to ask me to do that I'll have to insist that we take this indoors."

Brian laughs. "No. I don't think that will be necessary."

Kyle takes a few steps toward him. "I wanted to thank you again for what you did. I mean, I'm not living the high life yet, but you kept me moving, and I've made some friends. Things are looking up and that's all down to you, so. Thank you. Again."

Brian's chest fills with the satisfaction of a job well done, but also with a more personal contentment that he can't as easily define. It's just that he doesn't seem able to stop looking Kyle up and down, as politely as he can manage, memorizing the shape of his face and neck and shoulders, the way his pants hug his thighs, the cute, slightly pointy ends of his ears and—

"You're welcome," he replies, still smiling. "It was the right thing to do."

"Are you, uh, a doctor, then?" Kyle asks.

"I'm in school," he replies. "I'm studying to become a—" He wants to use the technical term but is afraid that it will make him sound pretentious. "Sort of a vampire doctor, I guess you could say? I, um, it's a lot to do with drugs, to be honest." He laughs, feeling stupid all of a sudden. This is usually where his introductory conversations with men end. "I prefer working with people one-on-one, but I haven't decided where I want to focus my efforts."

"Wow. That's—I've never heard of that before."

"It's new," he explains. "I mean, everything related to vampires is new. But especially this. We've only started to scratch the surface of the science behind it all."

"That's really amazing. I mean—I got the impression that anything you were involved in would be." Kyle swallows, and continues to close the distance between them. "I'm working on my ID so that I can register and do everything correctly." He smiles.

Brian can feel the warmth of him, so close now. "That's great. You said you made some friends. Did you, um, find a job, or...?"

"You could say that," Kyle answers, cheeks going pink.

Brian allows himself to look at Kyle as he would any patient. He's obviously been getting a steady supply of blood, and Brian isn't going to question that; there are plenty of willing donors, especially for young vampires whose powers aren't so developed that they intimidate people. With a blush, he adds silently, *And especially for the attractive ones.*

"May I ask you a personal question?" he asks, trying to divert his current train of thought.

Kyle licks his lips. "That depends. But go on."

"How old were you when you were turned and how much time has passed since then?"

"I was sixteen," Kyle answers. "It's been three years. I'm nineteen—you know, technically."

"That's—I'm interested in the aging question." Brian stares, enthralled, at Kyle up close, so pale, so young. "I mean, we've already proven that you do age—it's just so slow that it's almost unnoticeable. But the degree to which it slows differs from vampire to vampire, and even beyond that, it's affected by any number of conditions." He's doing it again. He slams his mouth shut, feeling heat pound in his cheeks. "I'm kind of a nerd," he admits breathlessly.

Kyle laughs. "I think it's adorable."

The way his eyes light up when he smiles, dimples deepening, teeth showing, crow's feet crinkling, god, he is so good-looking.

"Do you always work this shift?" he asks, and then rushes to add, "I only ask because I'd like you to do my registration. I—it's going to be under a different name."

"As long as you're only going to register here and let me handle your rationing, I'm willing to let it slide," Brian replies. He shouldn't. It's unprofessional. But he can't take it back now. "If you have the paperwork to back it up, I'm happy to work with you."

Kyle smiles, straightening as he reaches out a hand. "I'll come by when I have everything, then. Thanks."

Brian meets him in the middle. He shakes Kyle's hand, shivering at the way it feels in his, warm and strong. Theoretically he knows just how much power is lurking behind that grip—it's just that he's never had cause to make the observation personal before. With Kyle, he can't seem to stop making it personal. He also can't seem to stop blushing like a teenager.

"I'll see you soon," he says, half holding his breath.

"Um, yes. That's—goodnight," Kyle says, looking just as flustered.

"A lot of it is instinct," Clara says, without looking up from her laptop. Her fingers fly at a supernatural pace, so fast Kyle is amazed that the keys haven't started to fly off too.

He's going to observe his first customer appointment today and he's nervous. He's spent the last couple of weeks escorting people all over the building, helping with paperwork and getting lessons in anatomy and blood drawing from Janice, but there's no way to fully prepare for this kind of thing, as Elisa so often likes to remind him.

"I mean, when you're feeding, it's good to know the technical yada yada, don't get me wrong. It's good to eliminate as much trial and error as you can beforehand. But when you're doing it—when you're doing it, it's just right. It's what we're built for. Yes, the strength and the youth and the vitality and the speed are all kickass—but honestly? The only time that I feel truly myself is when I'm feeding on a human."

Kyle squirms, propping his toes up on the little stool in front of him. He's been giving himself a pedicure. It's the last step in cleaning himself up for the job, if you don't count putting on the outfit Elisa has asked him to wear.

"I'm just not crazy about the idea of being a predator, I guess," he admits.

"It doesn't have to be like that," Clara says. "Like any intimacy, it can be perfunctory, sexless—like a doctor's visit. Or it can be for pleasure, like sex without attachment. Or it can be everything all at once, like with a partner. It's—it can be a lot of things. It depends on your intentions. And your partner."

"And when it's not consensual?"

She frowns. "Then it's rape." She stares at him over the lip of her laptop. "And it's always dangerous, no matter how you're doing it. Killing like that, it's so easy. They'll fight you, of course, but taking life is nothing for us; we just overwhelm them. They go out like candles, snuffed out in seconds—" She pinches her fingers together. "A little hiss and a sag and they're meat."

She wets her lips. "Elisa once told me that you can't understand your nature until that happens, until you prove to yourself how lethal you can be. I don't know if that's true, but—we all come to understand ourselves in time, I think, mistakes or no mistakes. Just be smart. That's all you can do."

"But ever since turning I don't feel things the way I did before," Kyle says. "It's almost like, as time goes by, these gaps start forming. I used to be unable to imagine feeding on a human, and then suddenly I just could. I used to be sickened by violence, and then I started having dreams of nothing but. And sometimes, sometimes when I think of taking life, there's no reaction. Or there is one, but it's only because I force it."

Even now, the trauma of killing Jeffrey has receded to simple panic. He wonders if, in a year, he'll be affected by it at all.

He can't help but think about this side of himself, considering the way he's felt since meeting Brian; being so instantly and completely attracted to a human has presented him with a new challenge. He knows what it's like to act out violently, but what would it be like to be with Brian for pleasure? Would he feel all the things that humans feel when they're intimate? He never had the chance to experience this as a human.

"There's a lot of talk about that," she replies. "About how we can and do disconnect because in a medieval world we'd be hunting them, wouldn't we? But that's not this world. I think we have to find a balance. I think being happy is more important than understanding every little thing the moment we wish we could."

Kyle wonders if this is why she is so crazy about Elisa, who is the very embodiment of pleasure before business—or perhaps it would be more accurate to say that she's very good at turning pleasure into business.

He smiles, tilts his head at Clara and wiggles his toes, which are now painted with clear nail polish and looking rather fabulous, if he does say so himself. "I like your mind," he says, and winks at her when she laughs. "All right. I'm going to go put my evening gown on."

She smiles at him. "Go get 'em, tiger."

Brian smiles at Kyle through the glass as he takes the items Kyle has brought as proof of identification from the drawer.

"How was your seminar?" Kyle asks.

Brian laughs, self-consciously at first and then happily, shuffling the papers. "I think you're the only person who's asked aside from Erica." He looks sideways and then directly at Kyle, his mouth forming a happy purse. "It was excellent. Just, landmark, I mean, the first of its kind and—so many amazing minds, so much back and forth. It was kind of a mess at times, but it was thrilling. I think—I'm feeling good about the future, I guess."

Kyle's face is bright with secondhand happiness. "That sounds amazing. To have that kind of passion must be—I'm jealous."

"Are you planning to pursue anything at the moment, or...?" Brian blushes when he realizes that the question might be considered rude.

"I acted in high school before I was turned," Kyle answers, somewhat evasively.

Brian senses a sad story, there; though he's curious, he has no desire to overstep any further than he already has. He smiles apologetically. "Let me, um, make some copies and get you into the computer so I can print up your card."

"You okay?" Erica asks, as they pass each other in the back room.

"Yeah. Stressful night," he says evasively.

Before long he's got a laminated ID card with Kyle's picture on it in his hot hands and he delivers it with a smile. "Do you know roughly what time you'll make a habit of coming in?"

"How is midnight for you?" Kyle asks cheekily.

Brian laughs, high-pitched and sudden. He feels so very relieved. "That's perfect."

Now that Kyle has an identification card, there is no reason to see him in the examination room. Brian passes the blood over to him as he would to any vampire, though he keeps fidgeting, smoothing down his scrub top and adjusting the back of his hair. They've danced around each other for weeks now. Midnight on the dot, small talk through the glass. Erica smirking knowingly as she handles the other exchange window.

He knows that pretending this is just a professional exchange is silly—they're obviously interested in one another, but Brian isn't sure how it might pan out. He knows nothing about Kyle aside from a variety of details that form no larger picture. He knows Kyle must be in some kind of trouble, or he wouldn't have shown up at the center the way he did.

This always seems to happen to Brian—attraction before understanding, and disappointment when he realizes that most of what has drawn him to someone has nothing to do with reality and everything to do with wishful thinking. He's a hopeless romantic. He's fallen in love several times, far too quickly, only to be disillusioned once he's actually come to know the object of his affections. Ten to one Kyle will turn out to be another failed attempt, but knowing that has never stopped him from taking a chance before.

They're a few minutes into a conversation about Chicago nightlife one evening when Erica pokes him in the side as she walks past. She gives him a look that clearly says, "You are at work, you realize?"

"Look, um, we could continue this conversation when I get off, if you'd like," Brian says, trying not to sound too eager.

At almost the same time, Kyle asks, "May I take you to breakfast?"

They look at each other and laugh, eyes skidding sideways and cheeks flushing pink. Brian steadies himself. "I'd like that." He'll have to sacrifice a little sleep, but he's more than willing to do so.

"I'll meet you in the parking lot at seven-thirty?"

"Sure, that's—that would be perfect."

He manages not to let out a soft whoop until Kyle is out of the front doors.

"Finally," Erica moans. "I thought I was going to have to superglue your two clueless asses together."

Brian's heart is racing and he knows that he's grinning like an idiot. He punches the air, does a little spin and then freezes, grabbing Erica's shoulders. "He asked me out!"

"Yes, I noticed," she says, smirking. "I was there, remember?" The smirk morphs into a genuine smile. "Congratulations. Now get back to work, slacker."

"I had a feeling you were going to be a pancake man," Kyle says, crossing his legs.

Brian cuts his blueberry pancakes into pieces. "It's weird to be eating with someone who can't join me." He smiles, sipping his orange juice. "One day the synthetic blood will be so much more beneficial and affordable and they'll serve it everywhere."

"You don't have any vampire friends or family?" Kyle asks.

"My brother is a vampire," Brian answers. "Other than that, no, not really. This isn't the best impression to make, I guess, but I don't have many friends outside of school and work. My hours make a social life impossible when it comes to humans, and I always seem to spend more time serving vampires than befriending them."

"Business over pleasure?"

"Not really," Brian replies. "I'm a workaholic. And a bit of a nerdy hermit. I'm the kind of guy who enjoys medical textbooks, so—you can take that however you like."

Kyle laughs. "Have you always been interested in medicine?"

"God, no," he answers, wiping his fingers on a napkin. "I was a performer, sort of, like you. I even went to college to study the dramatic arts."

"Why the change of heart?"

Brian's throat closes up. He wets his lips and lowers his voice. "My mom got sick." He forces a smile. "It's a long, depressing story."

"My parents died when I was six. Car crash." Kyle's face closes off for a second, a flash of discomfort so keen that Brian wants to reach across the table and touch him. "My aunt and uncle raised me—and they made it very clear that they had no desire to take on the job. I also have long, depressing stories to tell." His eyes are glassy. He looks away, shredding a strip of straw paper between his fingers.

"So, there are tragic elements to our dramas," Brian says, smiling. "This is okay, right?"

Kyle's face is still guarded, but he nods. "I'm fine with it if you are."

"There's, um," Brian begins, trying to think of how to phrase it. He's been working up to this since they sat down. The segue feels heavy-handed, but he desperately wants to change the subject to something positive. "The Lyric Opera of Chicago is putting on *The Magic Flute*. It's one of my favorites. I haven't—I wanted to ask you if you would like to accompany me this Saturday?"

Kyle's cheeks go pink. He bites his lip and then releases it into a smile. "I'd love to."

*

What are they going to talk about if Kyle can't talk about himself?

This is the thought that keeps running through his head as he counts off the days until the weekend. It's the thought that absorbs him even as he takes customers: one after the other, men of every age, size, race and creed. He waits for one of them to present a challenge or do something to take him out of his own head. He could use the distraction.

It isn't until he is with a good-looking guy close to his own age that he finds what he's looking for. The customer is dark-haired and has a nice smile and—okay—he reminds Kyle of Brian, if he's being honest; trim but not over-muscled and soft in all the right places.

He sits on the couch in the visiting room. Kyle sits next to him and goes through the standard procedure of disinfecting the spot that he wants bitten. They've already done all the talking they have to do regarding the rules, and the testing to make sure he's clean has already been done downstairs.

"Could I put my arm around you?" the boy asks politely.

Kyle wants to hesitate but doesn't. "Sure."

He feels a warm, tentative touch at his lower back, an arm hooking around his hip. He shivers. He's never been touched like this before. It's not uncomfortable, but it is new. He swallows nervously, hiding his face in the boy's shoulder, letting his breath come faster.

The customer begins to whimper and he grows excited in response. It's like as if a switch is flipped; one moment he's trapped inside his own head, worrying and fussing, and the next he's fighting a racing pulse and mouthing wetly across the boy's shoulder. The almost innocent way his shirt is tugged down around his upper arm drives Kyle insane.

"Oh," the boy moans, and that—

Kyle makes a noise and kisses his neck. He draws on the skin and stares at it, finding the vein, making sure it's in a safe spot. He has to do this correctly, but it's so hard to think when he can hear the boy's heartbeat and feel the heat coming from his skin, the thrill coursing through him. This guy is anticipating him, aching for him. He can smell everything—the sweat and the arousal and the fear—and his fingers twitch and his throat clamps up and he needs this boy, he needs his blood and his pleasure and he needs it now. His fangs drop from his upper gumline and he feels them touch his lower lip.

"Please," the boy begs, and that's it; he can't wait any longer.

He holds the boy's jaw in one hand and bites down—the boy stiffens, and there is just something so sexy about that first shock of pain that makes them go rigid—and it's clean. Kyle's teeth are as sharp as surgical tools; all it takes is one smooth insertion to break the skin and the vein and he immediately withdraws. Doing so allows the blood to gush and gush it does, filling his mouth in jerky spurts. He drinks without allowing so much as a drop to escape.

As always, he loses himself in it. It's like free-floating in electricity-charged water, weightless, ecstatic, alive. In so many ways it's thoughtless; he just swallows and it's everything, without him needing to do a single thing to encourage it: warmth and taste and body and completion. Clara had been right. This is what they're made to do.

He can feel the boy twitching and sobbing against his fingertips, against his side. The boy's hand is closed around the back of his shirt and Kyle strokes his face, his neck and his shoulder to calm him as he writhes where he sits, enjoyment evident in every quivering line of his body.

Kyle pulls away when the boy begins to go limp, tonguing around the edges of his mouth to keep the blood from spilling. The blood around the puncture marks is already congealing. Kyle breathes heavily; he can feel how widely dilated his pupils are. His heart is racing.

"All right?" he asks, raspy and overwhelmed.

"Y-yes, thank you," the boy replies shakily.

They're not encouraged to linger afterward beyond making sure that the customer is okay to be left alone to recover, so he sees to the wound and leaves the boy with the usual—extra bandages, antiseptic, an iron supplement, a business card, a post-biting treatment guide and a receipt. He adds a smile and a handshake and calls it a job well done.

Back in his room he lies on his bed and allows himself to give in to it—drinking blood leaves him feeling a bit high, but it's never—it's never done *this* before and he's not quite sure how to feel. He stares down at the erection tenting his slacks and groans. He tongues coppery salt from the roof of his mouth, a tingle flickers across his body, and when he strokes a hand down over himself, it's not the boy from the appointment he thinks about.

✷

"I really think that Pamina stole the stage," Kyle insists, swerving them sideways around a couple walking a dog.

"I dunno, the coloratura certainly had some great moments," Brian counters.

"But they were just moments," Kyle replies, rolling his eyes fondly. "There's something to be said for a consistent performance."

They've been going back and forth about their favorite scenes from the opera for blocks now. It was amazing, of course—the theater and the lighting and the costumes and the voices, the color and the sound and the choreography. The intermission and the overpriced drinks and the way they'd held hands through the second act.

It's only when the conversation slows that Kyle realizes where he's leading them, and the beauty of the evening fractures.

It hadn't seemed like a big deal when Brian asked, "Do you live close? Can I walk you home?" He'd said yes without thinking, and now he's taking Brian not only to the place where he lives, but also the place where he works.

Will Brian understand the significance of the mark on the door? If he does, will he ask if Kyle works there or just lives there? And will Kyle tell him the truth or not? There is already so much unspoken between them; he doesn't want to add to the pile with a flat-out lie, but he can't help feeling a little embarrassed.

He holds his breath when they stop in front of the building.

Brian looks at the building and then at Kyle. "Your place?"

Kyle bites his lip and nods. "I had a wonderful time. It's been so long since I've—okay, so this is like the second time I've actually seen a real show in a real theater. It was perfect. You—just, thank you for a lovely evening." He can see that Brian's eyes are lingering on the reverse vampire symbol on the door, and he has to say something. "I work here."

"I figured," Brian says, tense and awkward.

Dread wells up in Kyle's chest. "Do you—does it bother you, that I do this for a living?" he asks, frowning.

Please don't judge me. Please don't hate me.

Brian slumps, his expression collapsing into concern. "Oh, god. Oh god, no. No. I just worry. Sometimes these places aren't safe, aren't—clean, and—"

"They're really strict, actually, about all of that," Kyle says, hating the way his voice catches as he rushes to defend the club. He can feel the space between them widen as if by miles. He wants to reach out, tangle their fingers and dispel the misunderstanding. "They're good people."

Brian stares at him, wide-eyed. "You don't need the blood from the center at all, then."

This brings Kyle up short. It isn't what he expected to hear next.

"No, I don't. I had other reasons for wanting to be there," he says, voice thick with emotion.

The smile that spreads across Brian's face at this confession breaks like a sunrise. He exhales all the breath in his lungs and closes the distance between them, cupping Kyle's face in his hands. He thumbs Kyle's cheekbones, breathes warm across his skin as the distance between them mercifully closes.

"God, Kyle," he sighs, bringing the pad of his thumb to Kyle's bottom lip.

"I have no idea what I'm doing," Kyle blurts, suddenly nervous. "I've never done this."

"Never dated, never...?" Brian's confused eyes search his. Kyle sees nothing judgmental in them.

"Never. Never been—" He stops talking, unable to continue. Brian is so close.

"Kissed?" Brian asks, breathless, as he leans in and presses their lips together.

"Never," Kyle replies, but the word is muffled by Brian's mouth and he is all too happy to let this state of affairs continue. The sensation consumes him.

Brian slides his fingers into Kyle's hair and deepens the kiss. They kiss again and again and again, warm and damp and hungry, holding each other close as the light from the droplet of blood on the vampire's fang logo glows behind them like a bloody halo.

Brian spends the morning cleaning his apartment in anticipation of Kyle's first visit.

His usual plan for this kind of date is to offer to cook a nice meal, but since that is out of the question, he'd suggested they marathon something cheesy on DVR and spend the night in. They've been doing the sweet-but-somewhat-impersonal-dating thing a while now, and he wants to slow down and get some more intimate conversation going.

At some point between dusting a bookshelf and dancing to the radio, a thought occurs. His blood type is Kyle's ideal nutritional match—would it be crazy to draw some for him before their date? He has everything he needs to do it in the apartment, even the liquid used to prevent the blood from coagulating.

He calls Michael when he fails to decide the matter for himself.

"It's rare that a vamp would turn that down. But offering your own blood is personal," Michael says.

"I really, really like this guy," Brian replies.

"You do? Good god, I had no idea. I am completely in the dark in regard to this topic. You haven't been talking about him nonstop for weeks, so how would I ever know? Why do you not communicate with me anymore, little brother? Hanging up on you now."

Brian laughs. "Okay. I get it."

"No, really. I am going to hang up on you. But I say go for it."

He juggles the idea all morning, but finally has to make a decision; he'll need an hour or two to recover from losing enough blood to fill even a minute portion of a champagne flute or wine glass (he's not going to toss one of those plastic packs at Kyle, at least not at this stage in the dating process), even with the supplement he has on hand to help recovery along. He rationalizes that this isn't the first time he's made a donation, and if he wusses out he can always just decide not to offer it to Kyle; so he goes ahead and draws blood.

By the time Kyle arrives, he's suitably dressed—designer jeans and a neat button-up—and acceptably recovered from the blood loss. Kyle wears fitted, dark purple pants and a red dress shirt with a black tie. His hair is perfect and he's practically glowing. Brian intends to compliment him, but all of a sudden he has an armful of him instead and the words die between their lips.

When they break apart with a damp smack, he sighs, tingling from head to toe. "Hello."

Kyle grins. "Hi."

"Come in."

Brian's apartment is in a nice neighborhood, but it isn't what one would call upscale. He's thankful that the money left to him by his mother had been more than enough to pay both his tuition and rent on something modest, but the sad truth is that he's not home much, and when he is, he's usually sleeping. He wishes he were around to enjoy it more, or to put more effort into the décor.

"Wow," Kyle says, laughing. "This is palatial compared to the space I have." He smiles, doing a turn in the center of the living room. "Not that I'm complaining, of course."

"I'm very lucky to have this place," Brian admits. "When my mother passed, she left me an inheritance. Otherwise I'd be shoulder to shoulder with the rest of the broke med students."

Kyle tilts his head. "Were you close?"

"In our own way," he replies, motioning for Kyle to join him on the couch. "We grew very close after she was diagnosed. I got pretty heavily involved in her treatment. Toward the end they offered to try turning her, to see if they could at least stop her kidneys and liver from shutting down and give the chemo more time to work, but it was too much. This was before it became common knowledge that turning doesn't heal existing conditions. People thought it would be like the old Anne Rice novels—that she'd just morph into this perfectly healthy version of herself. Not so much. Well. I sure know how to open up a romantic evening, don't I?"

Kyle's eyebrows are drawn together in sympathy. He puts a hand on Brian's knee. "God, no, it's all right. I want to know everything about you."

"What about you, you said your aunt and uncle raised you...?"

"If you can call it that," Kyle says, eyes going darker.

"Is that why you left right after graduation?"

"Um, yes. Exactly. I had to get away and I—I didn't want to go to the local community college. It would've just been high school part two, only worse. I ran out of options." He shrugs. "They would have wanted me out as soon as I started college, anyway, so I just cut to the chase."

"I'm sorry you had such a miserable time," Brian says, scooting closer.

"I'm having a pretty good summer, so we can postpone the pity party for now," Kyle says, the muscles of his face relaxing again.

Brian thinks about the wine glass he has waiting. He clears his throat. "Um, obviously I—are you hungry?" Kyle's eyes go very, very wide. "I drew some blood earlier," he says into the awkward silence. "I'm the right type. You don't have to drink it, of course, I just wanted to offer you something."

"That's very thoughtful of you," Kyle says, still looking stunned. "I'd—yes, please."

Brian starts the recording on the television while Kyle drinks. He tries not to stare, but it's a challenge. Kyle tips the blood from the rim of the glass into his mouth in careful, dainty sips. The insides of his lips are stained and he keeps licking out and fluttering his eyelids unconsciously and—Brian's face burns. There's something about this that makes his belly cinch tight with arousal. A part of him passing into Kyle, nourishing Kyle; it's more intimate than anything else he can imagine them doing together right now.

He takes the glass away when Kyle is finished and tries not to be too obvious about noticing how the blood changes him. He's flushed, his pupils have dilated and he's breathing off-rhythm. He looks blissful. He looks sexy. No—*sexual.* He always looks sexy to

Brian, but right now the distinction between idea and action is drawn clearly across his already-attractive features.

"May I go clean up?" Kyle asks.

"Second door to the left," he replies, and tries to calm down while Kyle rinses his mouth clean.

When Kyle returns they settle in front of the television, trading jabs and jokes about Brian's selection. He puts an arm around Kyle and Kyle scoots low to cuddle against his chest, tucking his head just under Brian's chin. It's a lovely feeling, being so close, made lovelier by the fact that it's not awkward in any way. Being with him feels right.

He realizes that Kyle is watching him and not the television. Kyle's pupils are still wide from the blood. Brian can't resist sliding a hand up along the back of his head and enjoying the feel of the bristle of hair against the grain. He traces the skin below Kyle's hairline and applies the slightest pressure to bring them closer together. The look on Kyle's face when their lips meet can only be described as relief.

"It was yours? Really?" Kyle asks between kisses, sliding up onto his knees.

"One hundred percent organic fresh-squeezed me," Brian answers, trailing his lips across Kyle's jawline. Kyle tilts his head and Brian takes it as an invitation to explore, pressing kisses from the hinge of Kyle's jaw to the softest part of his throat, where he can feel Kyle's pulse hammering against his skin.

"You tasted good," Kyle says, laughing. "Is that weird to say?"

Brian tongues the heartbeat pounding beneath his lips. "You taste good, too." He could linger here forever: Kyle's throat, Kyle's shoulders, Kyle's skin, all so impossibly beautiful.

"Oh," Kyle whines.

He licks a stripe across Kyle's collarbone, pausing to drop a kiss between the ridges. "Please tell me if I'm making you uncomfortable," he whispers, sinking his fingers deeper into Kyle's hair.

"I don't think uncomfortable is how I'd describe it," Kyle breathes.

And there it is again, that subtle throb of contained strength as Kyle's arms go around him. He knows that Kyle could crush him if he lost control of himself. The sensation that results from this knowledge skirts the line between fear and excitement so neatly, it's almost too much of both.

He kisses up the other side of Kyle's throat and jaw, finding and tugging an earlobe between his teeth and rubbing it back and forth with his tongue.

"God," Kyle moans.

They've been careful. They've taken things so slowly, hands above the waist, never letting things grow too heated—but this is the first time, they've been completely alone in private (brief trips up to Kyle's small bedroom at the blood club hardly count, what with the voices and music coming through the walls and Elisa knocking on the door every ten minutes just to mess with them), and it's impossible not to want more.

"You feel so good," Brian confesses, biting at his shoulder. He kisses Kyle again, twisting soft hair between his fingers—and flinches when pain flares hot and sudden across his mouth. He jerks back. His lip is bleeding.

Kyle pulls away. "Oh, my god. Sorry. My—" His fangs are distended.

Brian whimpers before he even realizes how he feels. "It's okay. We can cool off?"

Kyle is staring at his bloody lip. It's no worse than a paper cut, but it hurts and it's bleeding freely. Their eyes meet again and Brian breathes out, slow and careful. He stares at the elongated teeth, unable to stop himself; they're longer, sharper versions of human canines. He knows it would be silly to find them attractive, but there's something about them, long and bone-white and framed by Kyle's pink mouth, that makes his body ache.

Kyle drags a thumb across his lip, smearing the blood. He kisses Brian's lower lip, then sucks it in, careful to keep it ahead of his teeth. Brian shudders, warmth rushing across his skin, arousal clamping persistently on other very awake and interested places. Kyle licks the cut clean, breathy noises cresting low in his throat.

God, the way that *feels*—

"We don't have to cool off," Kyle says, nudging their noses together. "Unless I have sufficiently freaked you out."

Apparently not. Brian is surprised at his reaction. "Do it again?"

Kyle closes his lips and sucks on Brian's lip until it hurts. Brian lets it go on for several seconds after that, shaking as the pain lashes down his body. The cut throbs in time with his heartbeat. His head is spinning. He's beginning to get hard.

Kyle shivers and pulls away. Their foreheads touch. "I need a second, if—if we're going to stop this before it goes any further."

"Me too," Brian admits. They're both pretty far gone, and it happened so fast.

"The blood makes me kind of uninhibited. I don't want to make an ass of myself in front of you." He smiles self-deprecatingly. "I guess I'm doing that already. I just have no idea what I'm doing, and I like you so much."

"No," Brian replies, stroking his fingers down Kyle's back. He can't stop staring at Kyle's fangs. "You're worth taking the time for. I don't want to rush any of our firsts. I like you, too. So much."

"Okay," Kyle breathes, blushing pink.

Elisa comes to get Kyle for dinner, which she hasn't done in a while. When they sit down to their glasses, she slides a cell phone across the table.

"This is for you, okay? I'm tired of having to shout to get your attention; it is both boring and a waste of my valuable time." She knocks back a swallow of blood. "Also, I really enjoy the idea of having you at my literal beck and call, and I fully intend to interrupt your carnal relations with the doctor whenever possible."

"Thanks," he replies, smirking. "Is there a limit on minutes or texts or whatever?"

"Don't worry your pretty little head," she replies, crossing her legs.

"Could it be tracked?"

She carefully sets her glass down. Her hair tumbles around her shoulders as she leans forward, lowering her voice. "I'm not stupid, *gato*. If anyone comes looking I have no fucking clue who you are, and you know where the back door is."

"It's not just about me anymore," he explains.

"I know," she mumbles, waving a hand dismissively. "*El doctor*. Whatever you got, baby, you better work it—you wanna keep him close, huh?"

"He's amazing," Kyle sighs. "He cares and he likes me and he's romantic and smart and *hot*."

"I'm eating. Please. Spare me the details."

He laughs and plays with his napkin, watching shadows dance around the candles on the table. "To be honest, he's being a little too gentlemanly. I'm not sure how to let him know that I want more without sounding demanding."

"*Dios mio*," she sighs. "Don't play the blushing virgin. Tell him what you want. Take control of your fucking desires, okay? Be that shit. Trust me, it's the only way to live."

He supposes that she has a point.

They drink in silence for a while. She smokes a cigarette.

"I won't ask for details, mostly because I don't really care," she says, her face a red and brown smudge through the halo of cigarette smoke. "But it was bad, wasn't it?" Her voice is even: no condescension, no mockery, no curiosity.

"Yes," he replies. "It was."

He's intentionally avoided the news since he arrived, both on the Internet and on television, and only in the last few days has he even begun to consider reading the papers. He doesn't expect to see anything, but he hasn't been willing to chance it. He knows that at some point, most likely because of or for Elisa, Clara and Brian, he's going to have to start talking about it. But he isn't ready. Not yet.

She nods, blowing smoke. "It's a good thing you've got yourself a sugar daddy then, huh?"

He rolls his eyes.

"When the first manuals came out, they warned us to arm ourselves with wooden crosses and silver," Brian says, tossing his pencil and dragging two hands through his hair. "Some of the literature is still that outdated. How are we supposed to work with this garbage?"

He is sitting at Erica's kitchen table, swallowing mouthfuls of chicken and dumplings between violent scribbling jags. They're working on one of his summer assignments together. She'd been educated originally in human medicine and only switched to porphyrical medicine after her internship, so most of her knowledge comes from hands-on experience and is often more helpful than the textbooks.

"Half of the rules that the center has in place are ridiculous, too," he goes on, pushing his reading glasses higher on his nose. "And don't even get me started on the healing cells nonsense that's going around the hospital forum this week. You know they're going ahead with start-up trials on that synthetic cancer treatment? When Liz told me I almost crapped my pants. The foundation of that proposal has as many holes as it does words and you know they're going to exploit—"

"It'll be years before any of this makes sense in the larger scheme of things," Erica says, tapping away at her laptop. "Don't be too critical. You never know what they'll find."

"I know, I know. I just want—I want to understand it all now. I want to educate everyone *now* and it drives me crazy that they don't see the huge flaws in their proposals. So much wasted time, effort, and funding."

"You have to choose, you know. You can't go into research and still treat them hands-on, not full-time." She stops to stare at him, and something about her expression gives him pause. He lets his head down onto his folded arms. "I know." He sighs. "Sorry. I'm being an ass tonight. I'm just exhausted. Between seminars, schoolwork and the center I barely have any time for myself. Or sleep."

She grins, looking back down at the books. "Neither of us has time for anything but work. I can't remember the last time I picked up a newspaper or turned on the TV just to catch up with current events." Smiling playfully, she continues, "And speaking of current events, you forgot to mention a certain someone."

He takes a pull from his beer bottle and eats another dumpling. "I'm not kissing and telling."

"Oh, come on. Come *on*. Have you...?"

He scrunches up his face. "No. God, we've only been dating for a month."

She raises an eyebrow. "Sweet zombie Jesus, you're old-fashioned."

"Nothing wrong with that."

"No, there's not," she sighs. "But they do say that it's amazing."

"What, sex? Yes, I have had it. Thanks."

She laughs. "No, sex with vamps. All that strength and stamina. You're going to tell me that you haven't thought about it?" She grins. "He could bench-press you for hours, the implications alone are—"

He blushes, shifting food around on his plate, and cuts her off. "I have. Of course I have, I just—want it to be right."

"You're a good guy," she says, smiling at him, and winks. "You've also got way more self-control than I do. I would've climbed that like a tree on the third date."

He laughs, pointing a chopstick at her. "I'm watching you, Erica Szeto. You just remember that he's taken."

*

"Brian!" Kyle shouts, from a block away.

There's a blur—and he's standing right in front of Brian, grinning excitedly. He's never done that blazing-speed trick in front of Brian before and Brian laughs, surprised.

"Hey, you," he chirps, dragging Kyle in close and kissing him. "I finally managed to get you out into the sunlight. Are you going to be okay?"

"Yeah, I'll be fine. It's sort of like—you know when you don't sleep well and you just feel off for the rest of the day? It's like that. It's not severe or anything. No worries." He kisses Brian's cheek.

They do the rounds at Lincoln Park, choosing to spend most of their time at the zoo, and then take a walk down Montrose Avenue Beach. The breeze provides welcome relief from the afternoon heat.

Brian eats a quick snack at a food cart. "I wish you could join me," he says.

Kyle bends closer to his ear and whispers, "I dunno, you look pretty appetizing."

He's kidding, but Brian feels the innuendo all the way to his toes. He's not sure if Kyle is referring to a literal meal of his blood or a carnal nibble, but either way his body is very interested. He tamps the feeling down—it's difficult not to think about Kyle that way, now that they spend a good portion of their time together making out.

"There's so much to see here. We'd never cover a fraction of this place in one afternoon," Brian says.

"Plenty of time to see it all," Kyle replies, threading their fingers together.

It's not a long ride to the German pub, despite the traffic.

"They have a summer ale here that they brew themselves," Brian says, giddy as a boy as he slides into a booth at the back of the bar. It's empty enough to still be spacious, but a healthy lunch crowd is beginning to gather. "It's amazing." He orders one, and a meat platter to go with it.

Kyle spends twenty minutes watching, amused, as Brian devours the food and polishes off two pints of ale. His belly swells against the tight waistband of his jeans in a ridiculous fashion, and Kyle can't help but laugh.

"You are the cutest thing I have ever seen," he sighs, his chin in his hands.

"You're only saying that because I've gone a few hours without talking about pharmacology or the X-Men."

Kyle rolls his eyes playfully. "You have bratwurst on your sleeve."

"Oh, geez." Brian pulls a stain-treater stick out of his messenger bag and goes at the smudge.

"What *don't* you have in there?" Kyle asks. He's seen Brian pull everything from a mini-sewing kit to a flashlight out of that bag.

"Kitchen sink," Brian answers. "That's in the car."

Kyle giggles, then gives in and just stares some more, his heart in his eyes. He's really no good at resisting Brian's old-fashioned charm.

After lunch they take a long, leisurely walk, hands clasped. Once Brian recovers from the drinks he's had, they head back to the car.

"We could hit up that art gallery," Brian offers as they pull into traffic. "The showing is on for another hour or so. Or there's the movie theater. Or the revival theater."

They're holding hands over the center console. Kyle turns them so that his is on top. He inhales and then breathes out, "Could we maybe go back to your place?"

Please get what I'm saying, he thinks. He doesn't want to come off as either ungrateful for the lovely day or too forward, but he's been ready for a while now and he doesn't want to lose his nerve.

Brian glances at him, smiling, and squeezes his hand. "Okay."

Kyle's heart pounds all the way to Brian's apartment; the click of the door closing causes it to skip a beat. He's nervous, and yet his skin is hot and his clothing feels tight and itchy against his skin, and he just *wants*. He wants to put his hands on his boyfriend so badly.

Brian toes off his shoes and turns to look at Kyle over his shoulder. A flush of red is visible across Kyle's cheeks and his eyes are wide and wet. Brian asks, husky and unsure, "Shower?"

Oh, my god, you can't just say *that.*

Kyle has no idea how foolish he looks standing there so aroused it hurts, his hands curled into fists and his chest heaving. "God, yes, please."

In the hallway outside the bathroom, Brian catches Kyle around the waist as Kyle reaches for him at almost at the same time, putting his hands on Brian's shoulders and then around the back of his neck, pulling him forward into kisses that start out soft but go hard within moments, tongues and teeth dancing around throaty noises that die before they are born.

It takes every bit of focus Kyle has to keep his fangs tucked away.

He pins Brian against the wall beside the bathroom door, carding fingers through his hair and turning his head up and back. His lips find the softness of Brian's throat and the hard ridge of his Adam's apple. He tugs Brian's button-up from the waistband of his jeans with falsely brave fingers, enduring a full-body shiver when Brian lets him undo the buttons one by one before shrugging out of the shirt. His undershirt follows and then they slow down, Kyle's lips hovering over his, his fingertips poised above the button on Brian's jeans.

"Want to see you," Kyle breathes, "all of you. Is that okay?"

"Of course, god, yes, anything you want, honey, *anything*."

He tongues the corner of Brian's mouth, undoing the button and zipper on Brian's pants and peeling the material down. He crouches, and his breathing accelerates ; Brian's dark body hair is neatly trimmed except for a thick trail that begins at his navel and ends at the waistband of his briefs, which—leave nothing to the imagination. Kyle kisses Brian's belly to stop simply gawking. He curls the briefs down and off, trying not to react visibly as Brian's cock rises in front of his face. He stands, shaking with the desire to touch, and is pulled into a heated kiss.

"Can we start the shower before I reciprocate?" Brian's eyes drift over him hotly.

He blushes. "Sure."

Inside the bathroom, Brian fiddles with the hot and cold shower settings and finally returns to Kyle's side, wetting his lips as he puts his hands on Kyle's hips. He kisses Kyle's neck and begins undoing the buttons on his shirt.

"You are so stunning," he says, pushing the cloth from Kyle's shoulders. His fingers trace the exposed skin, savoring it with a touch as he kisses along Kyle's chest. His hand finds the laces that hold Kyle's pale yellow pants closed. He picks them loose one by one and flattens his hand over the bulge that's straining against them.

Kyle writhes forward, breath abandoning his lungs in a rush. "*Brian.*" "Will you let me take care of you?" he asks, rubbing Kyle's erection through the laces. "Let me make you feel good?"

The urge to move, to do something, is so overwhelming that Kyle has to clamp down on every muscle. Part of him just wants to grab Brian, pin him against something and ravish him, but that's not what all of him wants. The part that matters today, the part that is really *Kyle*—young, inexperienced Kyle—wants Brian to pick him apart instead, layer by layer.

"Please," he moans. "Please touch me, please—"

Brian works the skin-tight pants and underwear off Kyle's legs and draws him into the shower.

The water feels heavenly after a day outside in the heat, and Brian set the water temperature at just above tepid, which is perfect. They soap up quickly and separately but can't stop staring at each other's bodies. Brian is hard now and Kyle wants to touch him so badly, but he's also very glad to have a chance to peek without having to do anything—it gives him the time he needs to calm down about both his own nudity and *their* nudity. Except for a high school locker room and Internet porn, Kyle hasn't seen another man naked, and he certainly hasn't been naked *with* one.

Once they've rinsed off, it's Brian who guides Kyle back against the cool tile, Brian who holds Kyle and kisses him and suckles his nipples to rosy, hard peaks before licking water from his chest and ribs as he sinks to his knees on the bathmat.

"Oh, god, oh—I—"

Brian sucks a kiss into his hip, eyes on his. "May I...?"

"Please." His cock is embarrassingly vertical, straining tight and shiny at the head as Brian kneels up higher and—licks at it, kisses it, then wraps his lips around it and sinks all the way down in one smooth motion. "*Oh my god.*"

The noise as Brian swallows and then pulls off, wet and clinging, is too much; Kyle can't control the forward snap of his hips, a wordless, needy reply. Brian finds a rhythm, his tongue and lips settling into sharing the task, and Kyle has to close his eyes and just focus on not coming instantly because—that *mouth*. Those plump lips and that eager tongue and god, he is doomed, so doomed—if *this* is the first blowjob, he's not sure how he's going to survive everything else.

He gasps and laughs, overwhelmed and vibrating as Brian's slick dark head bobs and bobs and bobs. It feels so ridiculously good.

"I'm—going to—" His fingers settle on Brian's hair.

Brian pauses long enough to reply in a husky voice, "I know," before wrapping his fist back around Kyle's cock and closing his mouth hungrily around his head.

"Oh, *god*," he growls, feeling the strength surge in his hands and holding it back as he cups Brian's head, pushes forward and comes so hard that it almost hurts. Slick, noisy swallowing and Brian lifts off, sucking in a breath and licking at his friction-burned lips.

"Bed," Kyle moans, not caring that he sounds like a dying whale.

"Bed, please."

They kiss and towel off the whole way, Brian teasing him, "I had no idea that I'd be able to make that much of a dent in your stamina."

"It's not that," Kyle growls, grabbing Brian around the waist and—just lifting him and depositing him on the bed. "I only need more of you."

Brian stares, stunned, and leans back on his hands.

"Um," Kyle says, standing there with a towel around his waist, his long, pale body freckled with water droplets. The setting sun coming in through the windows feels warm against his naked back. "Was that not okay?"

Sometimes he forgets just how strong he is.

"That was very okay," Brian rasps, eyes raking over Kyle's body. "Lose the towel?"

Kyle swallows and drops it, blush-painted from his cheeks to his chest, as Brian stares at him, his eyes roaming slowly and deliberately over Kyle's body.

"Do you have any idea how beautiful you are?" Brian's cock is as hard as it was when they got into the shower, and it arches back toward his belly button. As he stares at Kyle, the head grows dark and smears a damp streak just under his bellybutton. Kyle's mouth goes dry. "Do you have any idea how much you turn me on?"

After a beat of silence, Kyle kneels on the floor between Brian's knees. He could respond, he could *ask*, he could talk about how he's never done this before, but none of that feels right and Brian already knows. So instead, he reaches out and wraps his fist around Brian's erection; it's shorter and thicker than his and has an odd taper, but he doesn't think much about that. He adjusts his grip and begins pumping it, his heart slamming in his chest.

"Oh, oh god, this is going to be over so fast if you keep doing that," Brian moans.

"I can go slower." He licks his lips nervously.

"No, it's just—it's just you—on me, touching me—I fantasized about this so many times, your hands, your beautiful hands, making me feel so good."

Kyle blushes, feeling a rush of pleasure at the idea that being himself, doing this, is enough to make Brian happy. It's not so scary when he knows without a doubt that Brian can be as satisfied by him as he is by Brian. The approval is like a drug, almost, making his head spin. He's never felt anything like this before, not even while drinking blood.

He kisses along Brian's inner thighs as his hand explores; it's really quite something, the beautiful cock in his hand, its bumps and ridges and the way the head flares, and he allows his fingertips to find each shape, to trace and press into the slit a little, then fall back to find the shaft once again. He kisses as high as Brian's balls and licks across them tentatively. They're smooth and crinkly and so delicate, and he loves the way they feel, so he does it again.

He begins to realize just how long it's been since he first realized that he was gay and started fantasizing about this, a man's cock in his hand, in his mouth, the way a man would smell and sound and feel, so good, so *right*.

Brian's hips rock, his cock sliding in and out of Kyle's grip. His belly heaves as he gasps and breathes and whines, up on his elbows watching Kyle kneel, touching him, in a pool of blurred orange sunset.

Kyle begins to pull faster. The give of Brian's silky hard cock is perfect in his hand.

"I'm," he whimpers, "I'm close."

"It's okay," Kyle replies breathlessly, "it's okay, just—let go, I want you to—"

Brian's whole body tenses and his hips pump harder, pushing his cock in and out of Kyle's fist, and then there's—come, everywhere, spurting hard and high over Brian's chest and belly and gushing lazily over Kyle's knuckles.

God, he *did that*. Of course, now that he's done it, he's not quite sure what to do with the result. He thought he'd be grossed out by the mess, but all he feels when he gazes down at his smeared hand is curiosity and arousal. He licks the back of his knuckles, shivering, unaware that he's being watched until Brian groans out loud at the sight.

"Salty," he comments, a grin curling his lips.

Brian is shaking, his cock still throbbing on his stomach as it shrinks and softens. He shifts up onto the bed fully and holds out a hand. "Come up here?"

Kyle crawls up onto the sheets, aware that his own cock is on its way to full hardness again. Touching Brian is so hot he can't say he's surprised. He straddles Brian's waist and bends down to kiss him.

Brian's hand finds his cock hanging heavy and half-stiff between his legs. "God, so soon—"

"Can't help it," Kyle whines, rutting down against the friction.

"I am not complaining," Brian replies. "Not too sensitive?"

"No, I'm fine." He kisses Brian's neck, Brian's chest, Brian's face. "I just want your hands on me. I just want *you*."

Brian rolls them over so that Kyle is under him, folding their bodies together. It's the first time they've really relaxed all day, and it feels good, even better as Brian takes his time mapping Kyle's face and shoulders with his mouth before sliding down the bed.

"What do you want, honey?" He licks a stripe across Kyle's hip. "My mouth?"

"Please, yeah." The promise of having that mouth around him again makes his cock twitch eagerly. He cards his fingers through Brian's hair. "Please, s-suck me again."

Saying that has the desired effect; Brian groans, tongues Kyle's cock into his mouth and sinks down, making Kyle's eyes roll back. Kyle's fingers tighten in his hair. Brian is warm and damp from the shower, and he looks so natural sprawled between Kyle's thighs. Kyle goes completely loose, lets the bed support his body and melts into the feeling of Brian's mouth around him.

There's something so lazy and wonderful about this second time. He isn't ready to explode after just a minute or two, and Brian not only finds a pace he hadn't managed to find before, he also seems to just open up, letting Kyle deep into his mouth and once or twice even into his throat. His face is a mask of arousal and concentration, as if sucking Kyle is the beginning, middle and end of his current universe. He's so focused, so obviously enjoying himself, and god, the noises—the wet, sucking noises from Brian taking his cock. It's all Kyle can hear above the pounding of his heart.

He spreads his legs wide and folds them out side to side to make it easier, but stops suddenly in surprise when Brian cups his thighs and then the swell of his ass, pulling him in deeper.

"Brian," Kyle gasps. He feels Brian's throat close around him again and again. "Oh god I can't—s-stop, or I'll—" But he doesn't stop, or he won't, and Kyle comes in his mouth with a sob.

He stays down there for a short while, licking until it's too much and Kyle has to beg him to really and truly stop.

Grinning, he crawls up the bed and settles next to Kyle. "Okay?"

"Dead," Kyle sighs, closing his eyes. His muscles still twitch all over and he's forgotten what it feels like to breathe evenly. When he can actually imagine mobility again, he rolls onto his side, curling his arms around Brian. "That was amazing."

"Which, the first or the second time?" Brian asks cheekily.

Kyle swats him, laughing. "Bad." He kisses him. "Everything. This whole day. You. Thank you for making it special."

"Thank you for being with me," Brian says, tangling his fingers in Kyle's hair. "I don't think I've ever been this happy." His voice catches on "happy" and Kyle's throat closes up.

This is more than he'd ever hoped for.

Brian attends a medical conference in New York at the end of the month. It's a three-day commitment, one he's been anticipating all summer. He's giving a presentation on the effects of the consumption of substance-laced human blood on vampires, focused specifically on accelerants. It's a hot topic this year; a study was published in early January that made some very out-there claims, and the medical journals have been tossing research and speculation back and forth ever since. A lot of Brian's research has focused on this topic, so he was an easy choice to fill one of the panel slots.

He doesn't think that he and Kyle are quite ready for a weekend away together. It's too soon, and Kyle would be bored; Brian will be with colleagues when he isn't speaking or attending talks; they wouldn't get to do or see anything together anyway. So he doesn't ask and, when Kyle smiles and shrugs and kisses him goodbye, he figures that it's not the end of the world for them to have a few days apart. They've been in each other's pockets so deeply lately. He knows that things are getting serious for him, but he isn't as sure about Kyle's feelings. There's a wall he hasn't been able to scale.

Alone in his New York hotel room after he's said goodnight to Kyle over the phone, he takes the time to really think about about his feelings for Kyle and the wall between them.

He has never met anyone quite like Kyle before—someone who fits him as if he were made to. Someone who shares many of his passions but who also has his own. Someone who appreciates the things about him that even he doesn't care for. Someone he can imagine sharing his life with on a long-term basis.

The most shocking thing about all this is how *not* shocking it is. Being with Kyle feels like the most natural thing in the world. Just a day or two away from him has already created such a physical longing for him it feels like a muscle that won't stop spasming.

On the last night of the conference, he calls Erica to check in about work. The first thing he says once business is taken care of is, "I think I'm falling for Kyle."

"Oh, sweetie," she croons.

"It's never felt like this before. I mean, I thought I knew; I have tried so many times with so many guys." He breaks off, frustrated. "But now it's all—uh, it feels too good to be true. Being away from him has made me realize how much I've come to want him around."

"But that's great. It's going well, right? The feeling is totally mutual, I'm sure."

Brian falls silent for a moment. "I think he feels strongly for me. But there's—there's something else. Something he hasn't told me. I can tell. We've never talked about why he came to Chicago with no plan or resources. Something drove him here, and I don't think the reason he gave me is the whole story."

"Here's a dumb suggestion." *And by dumb she means smart.* He smiles to himself. "Ask him."

"I don't want to scare him away."

"If it's bad enough for him to have kept it from you this long, then you might not want to be with him, right? So ask now, before you get in any deeper."

She's right, of course. But it's the last thing on his mind when he gets home. When he lands he texts Kyle, hoping that he will be available to at least come over for dinner, if not to stay the night. Brian has tomorrow off, and he wants nothing more than to be with Kyle until he has to go back to work. That thought is all that keeps him going on his way home from the airport, but the last thing he expects to find when he finally arrives is Kyle sitting outside his apartment door.

"Kyle?" He drops his luggage, emotion surging up in his chest.

Kyle is dressed in a swath of bright colors and black boots. In the time it takes Brian to say his name, he blurs forward supernaturally fast—it's a weird thing, being charged at that speed—and sweeps Brian up into his arms.

"Hey," Kyle exhales. Brian's legs are around his waist, and Kyle holds him up without any effort.

"Did you get my—"

"Um, yeah. But I was already here." His voice is rough. He lifts his head from Brian's neck and breathes out harshly, almost *hungrily*.

All Brian's thoughts of confronting Kyle about his past vanish as they kiss. Kyle's effort to hold back his strength is obvious in the trembling of his muscles. His kisses are so hard that they bruise, and Brian can feel the bumps against his lip where Kyle's fangs are trying to descend.

A thrill courses through him. He wraps his arms around Kyle's neck and threads his fingers through Kyle's hair. It's strange, being held up like this for so long without the other person tiring.

He shudders when Kyle's tongue slips inside his mouth, when Kyle's hands slide down to cup his buttocks and haul him higher, closer. He traces the fang bumps along Kyle's gumline with the tip of his tongue in reply.

Kyle growls low and cat-like and pulls back. "*Don't*. That—god."

"Did I hurt you?"

"The opposite," Kyle says. His pupils have dilated, leaving only a sliver of blue ringing a sea of black. "I'm okay, just—that does something to me, I can't even describe it."

"Let's get inside," Brian says, dropping his legs from Kyle's waist.

He doesn't realize how tightly Kyle has been holding onto him until he's released and can feel the sore places where bruises will inevitably form. He bites his lip, his cheeks darkening. He's never realized before just how much of a thing he has for being manhandled.

Kyle crowds him back against the door the moment they're through it, the combined weight of their bodies slamming it shut behind them. Kyle touches him, running his fingers along the back of Brian's skull, his legs trapping Brian's body between his own and the door. He kisses Brian until neither of them can breathe properly, and Brian finds the fangs with his tongue again.

"*Brian*," Kyle whimpers.

He can't help but smile; he knows that he's being a tease. "Missed you so much."

He doesn't often focus on the things that make Kyle different from him, but something about the way Kyle loses physical control when he gets excited makes Brian's heart race. Something about a young man who looks as if a stiff wind could knock him over, but who, in reality, could pick him up and toss him around like a rag doll—

If liking that is weird, Brian is happy to be weird.

"I missed you, too," Kyle says, palming Brian's jaw and kissing his neck. "Thought about you the whole time." He shivers, laving his tongue over Brian's collarbone and then back up to where his neck and shoulder meet. The skin there starts to go numb—not completely, but enough to tingle as if it is falling asleep.

"Oh, that's—"

"I know," Kyle says apologetically. "I can't help it." He swallows. "I mean, it only happens when I—when—I get excited. Sorry. Just, missed you."

"You—you can." Heat pounds in Brian's cheeks.

Kyle goes still, panting against his skin. "W-what?"

"You can, if you want," Brian repeats. All of a sudden, his body aches for something new, for something *more*, for something they haven't done yet. He can feel his cock slowly fill with blood simply at the idea—it has been rising since they started kissing, but now it's pressing insistently against the front of his jeans. "You can."

"Have you ever—"

"No," Brian answers.

It's impossible to think clearly with Kyle holding him against the door, with Kyle's head bent over his neck like this. He's so hard that his jeans are starting to hurt; the angle at which he's risen against them is uncomfortable, but he can't move. "Please." The anticipation is like ants beneath his skin, crawling and crawling and crawling. "*Please*."

Kyle kisses the half-numbed skin just inches from Brian's neck. His fangs are fully distended now and Brian can feel them, smooth and hard as they brush his skin.

The need to feel the pain he knows he'll feel, to feel opened, to feel his blood run past Kyle's eager lips, is sudden and new. Kyle can and will drink from his body; Brian can let him do it; this is a thing they can do *together*, and it is as exciting as it is frightening.

"You can," he repeats. He feels dizzy. "I want you to. Want to take care of you, please. Do it." His hands shake so hard that he can't even maintain a grip on Kyle's waist, but it doesn't matter; Kyle is supporting him.

"God," Kyle breathes, trembling, his lips damp as they pass over Brian's shoulder again and again. "Ever since you—that night with the wine glass, I—god, I've dreamed of your blood so many times."

"Please," Brian hisses, arousal pounding through his body. "Do it. *Do it.*"

Kyle's hands are so hard when they hold him, now. One cups his head and the other finds the middle of his back. The embrace feels different. It's an expression of Kyle's knowledge that, when he bites down, Brian will thrash, at least a little; it's a prelude to sensations that Brian won't be able to escape. Kyle is going to hold him still and make him *take it.*

He whimpers, anticipation making his muscles tense when Kyle's fingers tighten.

It doesn't hurt as much as it would without the numbing, but it still aches when Kyle bites, a deep, penetrating pain that Brian can feel in his bones as the fangs sink into his flesh and dig in hard. They withdraw seconds later, Kyle groaning as he closes his lips around the wound.

Once the first wave of pain passes, he can't help rubbing against Kyle; the burn of the bite is like the throb of an extra pulse beneath his skin, and he's so hot and it feels so good, like a hand on his cock, only *everywhere* at once. He gets Kyle's thigh between his and rocks against it wantonly. He's painfully hard and Kyle is like a wall against him, immovable and supportive. He loses himself rutting against Kyle, floating atop waves of ever-diminishing pain, so gone that he doesn't even feel his orgasm until it's right on top of him. He cries out when he feels himself tense—too late—and come in his pants with a choked-off sob.

And then the blood loss starts to assert itself. He slowly goes limp, flashes of numbing cold and panicky heat alternating in waves through his body, a sensation that's only made more intense by his post-orgasmic state. Kyle is still swallowing, noises cresting in his throat as he drinks and moans and drinks and moans. Black spots swim in front of Brian's eyes and he starts to sink. Kyle is the only thing holding him up against the door now.

Kyle gasps and forces himself to stop; there's blood on his lips and teeth and tongue and chin. Brian's eyelids flutter weakly as he stares at the color, so vivid against Kyle's pale skin. He's so tired all of a sudden. This is his last thought before he passes out.

He wakes up in bed. Kyle must have washed him, because he's clean all over and wearing his favorite pajamas (a pair of sweatpants he's had since high school and a university T-shirt worn so thoroughly there are holes under the arms). He feels as if he'd been run over by a freight train, but in a good, sexually satisfied, muscle-burn kind of way. Kyle is cuddled between his legs, his cheek on his stomach.

"Hey," he croaks, concern and affection in his tone.

"Hey," Brian answers.

"Take this," Kyle says, offering him a small handful of pills. Restoratives: iron, a vitamin—standard stuff, all of which Brian recognizes and all of which they've discussed before. He knocks them back with a swallow of water and then lies back down, boneless.

"Thanks." He smiles, eyes closed. Feeling Kyle warm against him settles him in a way nothing else could.

There's something about the blood loss, too. He feels unstrung and content; it felt amazing, which he hadn't expected. But it's not just physical. Feeding Kyle has left him with a sense of purpose and accomplishment. It's an extra bond between them, only possible because he is human and Kyle is a vampire. Not only can they sexually satisfy each other, Brian can also give Kyle the blood from his veins—the one thing he needs to live. It's a heady sensation.

"How are you feeling?" Kyle asks, propping his chin up on Brian's belly. "I thought maybe I went too far."

"I'm okay." The restoratives are prescription strength and have begun to work immediately.

"I don't think I'll pass out again. I was just—it was my first time."

Kyle's cheeks go pink. "I've never felt that level of response before." He lowers his voice, which has gone rough again, and traces shapes across Brian's chest with his fingers. "You came so fast." He turns a blushing cheek against Brian's belly. "Your whole body was shaking."

Brian inhales, feeling his pulse stutter. "It felt amazing for me, too." He exhales. "I feel so *loose* right now. Like after a massage or a hot shower."

"It's not like losing blood normally," Kyle says. "Elisa tried to explain it to me once. That it's—our saliva has all sorts of effects on you once it gets into your bloodstream. I guess you already know all this, huh?"

"Mm, some," Brian hums, carding his fingers through Kyle's hair. His brain is as lazy as the rest of him right now, and science is the last thing on his mind.

The hand Kyle has rested on Brian's thigh slides between them, and his thumb rubs along the inner softness. It inches up suggestively, and Brian can't help but smile.

"I am definitely done. At least for a while. But if you'd like to come up here..." He tilts his head, his tongue dragging over his bottom lip. "I'd love to return the favor." Kyle spreads out next to him but he shakes his head, brushing his lips across Kyle's ear and whispering, "Kneel over my chest?"

"Oh," Kyle breathes. "Okay."

Brian is so relaxed, he feels as if he could do anything right now. When Kyle settles with one knee on either side of his torso, he shifts lower. Kyle is wearing pajamas, too, so all Brian has to do is encourage him to take off his tank top—

"God, look at you"

—and peel his shorts from his sharp hips. His beautiful, long, pink cock bobs in the air, damp at the tip and flushed, curving upward. Brian's mouth actually waters at the sight.

"Put your hands on the headboard." Kyle does, and Brian slides his lips over his teeth and wraps them around the head of Kyle's cock. He hums appreciatively, hunger rising in him for more of that thick flesh.

When Kyle doesn't move, he pulls off and says, "You can use my mouth, okay?"

"Oh, god, I—"

This time when Brian puts his mouth back where it belongs, Kyle begins thrusting forward in short jabs that change Brian's intended angle, poke Brian's cheeks from the inside and even find the roof of his mouth before they decide on a rhythm. Brian sucks greedily, then, loving the pass of Kyle's cock over his tongue, loving every tangy drop of pre-come that dissolves there.

Kyle hovers over him, heavy and long, his thighs flexing as he gives in to it, as he fucks Brian's mouth, his balls tapping Brian's chin with every thrust. It feels good; Brian's throat and jaw are so relaxed, and Kyle quickly sheds his concern about pushing too deep when Brian proves that he has no trouble taking it. Brian whimpers, his mouth full, and digs his fingers into Kyle's buttocks, holding him there. Eventually, Kyle pulls back so Brian can suck in a breath.

"*God*," Kyle hisses. "So good at that, oh my god." His whole body trembles.

"Love you in my mouth," Brian breathes, mouthing the glistening, swollen tip. "Love the way you taste." He arches his neck. He wraps his fingers back around Kyle's cheeks and tugs. "Don't stop."

Kyle uses one hand to guide himself back between Brian's lips. He exhales, his head falling back. "I'm close, I'm so *close*. W-wait."

Brian squeezes his balls gently, traces two fingers across the space between his cheeks. Kyle freezes. "Let me...?"

"What—"

"It'll feel so good."

"In—inside?"

"Not yet, just—spread a little for me?" Brian presses two fingertips to the skin behind Kyle's balls and begins rubbing in firm, slow circles. "Relax, okay?"

"Oh," Kyle breathes. "*Oh*, that feels nice." He whimpers as Brian continues to stroke him. "Brian. Brian, that—oh, god, I'm going to—" Brian fists Kyle's cock and pushes against the spot, fast and sure. "*Shit*. Shit, shit, shit."

"Yeah," Brian breathes, jerking him harder. "Yeah, feels good, I know, feels so good." He's so aroused watching Kyle fall apart that he thinks he might be ready for another go sooner than anticipated. "If we—when I'm inside of you, sweetie, I'll be touching you there, I'll make you feel so good, I promise—I'll fill you up *so well*."

Kyle gasps. "C-coming—"

Flushed, he shakes as he shoots long stripes of white all over Brian's chin and mouth, bent over him as if his body can't take the intensity. He twitches for a long while after he comes, his eyes open and staring down at Brian's messy face.

"Oh god, sorry."

"Not a problem." Brian licks at the corner of his mouth, grinning. "I am so glad you were here to completely derail my romantic-night-in plans."

Kyle frowns, curling up against Brian's side as they clean off. "I didn't mean to."

"No, I meant that." He smiles, tipping their noses and lips together, breathing contentedly into a kiss. "I missed this as much as I missed everything about you." He glances sideways sheepishly, sliding an arm around Kyle's waist. "I have tomorrow off, if you're free. We could catch a movie or something. Interested?"

"I have a few appointments, but they're all later at night," Kyle replies, yawning as he tucks their limbs together and buries his face in Brian's hair.

Brian has a lot of material from the conference to sort, format and distribute, but it can wait a day. He closes his eyes and lets the comforting solidity of Kyle's body beside him lull him to sleep.

*

Kyle stares down at the plate of food on the counter and frowns. It looks and smells the way that he thinks it should, but it's been years since he's cooked or even really noticed human food, and it isn't as if he can taste it. Human food—both going down and, inevitably, rapidly back up again—isn't pleasant, and even if he were to just chew it, it wouldn't do him any good; his tongue no longer processes taste the way it did when he was human.

He wanders through the bedroom, mentally preparing an excuse that he's looking for his socks to justify stopping for a moment to watch Brian sleep. He's beautiful when he's that deep under, content and dreaming, and looks years younger than he is. Kyle smiles at him, feeling emotion flood his throat and chest. He is head over heels for this man.

He sits on the bed, pressing a kiss to the side of Brian's head. "Honey?"

"Mmph," comes the muttered response.

"Brian," he says, grinning, and then sings, "Bacon."

"Good morning," Brian replies, rolling over.

"Oh, I see how it is. Kisses, no. Bacon, yes."

"No way," he answers, taking Kyle into his arms. "Kisses and bacon are both very much a yes." He grins. "I could get used to this."

"Your breakfast is getting cold," Kyle informs him, touching their noses together.

Brian kisses him, voice sleep-rough and warm. "Can I be your breakfast instead?"

Kyle groans. "Food. You need it; you're tired, you've lost blood, and your stomach is empty—hands!"

Brian pulls away, smiling. "Okay, okay. I give up." He scrunches up his face. "For now."

With a silly smile on his face, Kyle watches him eat the eggs, bacon, fruit and juice that he's prepared. Then he watches television, half paying attention and half lost in thoughts of last night while Brian showers and catches up on a few work-related emails and voicemails. Brian joins him on the couch when he's finished, eagerly reaching for him.

"I can go, if you need to work," he says, cuddling against Brian's chest.

"Nah. Just had to take care of a few things that I should have last night."

"How—how often can we, um, do that?" Kyle asks, embarrassed.

He is doing everything he can *not* to look at the wound on Brian's neck—a faint set of bite marks, with two dark punctures where his canines broke the skin, surrounded by a ring of bruises of varying colors where he had sucked so hard he broke blood vessels. Seeing it sends a protective, possessive feeling through him. He reaches out and thumbs it softly. Brian shivers, licking his lips.

"The general school of thought is no more than twice a month," he answers. "But with the access I have to prescription strength restoratives, we could probably manage once a week without too many side effects. I'm your preferred blood type, so that helps; you can take less and it would be just as good for you."

Kyle feels his gums tingle at the thought of doing it again. God, he already wants it again—and that's not possible. He smiles instead of saying anything too revealing and tangles their fingers.

"Tell me about your conference," he says, and Brian grins.

"Really?" Erica asks, her voice flat and dry.

"What?" Brian counters.

"A turtleneck?"

He usually wears them under his long-sleeved scrubs in the winter. When the concealer hadn't quite done the job this morning, he'd had to resort to drastic measures. He deflates under Erica's scrutiny. He is, quite possibly, the worst liar on the planet.

"I was cold?" he tries.

"You didn't," she breathes, sounding delighted.

He'd hoped to make it through lunch without her noticing (though he's not sure what he'd pinned that hope on; she's been giving him looks all morning). "Erica—"

"Tell me everything! Come on, some of us don't get to date a *Cullen*."

"Okay, just for that, your cookies are forfeit. Hand them over."

Sighing, she passes him the packet. "Tell me *something*. Was it awful, did it hurt, are you okay?"

He's blushing already.

He can't tell her that it felt amazing in ways that blood loss should not. He can't tell her that he came in his pants like a fifteen-year-old, riding Kyle's thigh. He can't tell her that the moment it was done, he felt bonded to Kyle in a way he had never imagined. He can't tell her that he spent the entire next day stealing glances at the bite mark whenever he passed a reflective surface. He can't tell her that after Kyle had gone home, he had sat on his sofa and touched the tender mark until he grew so hard he had to jerk off to make the urgency subside. He can't tell her that he's already marked next week on the calendar so that he knows exactly when they can do it again.

"It was nice," is all he says, smiling into his soup cup. "It was just really nice."

The second person with whom he can't seem to avoid discussing his relationship with Kyle is his brother, who must have finally noticed how long they've been dating and how giddy Brian is, because he demands over the phone one evening, "So when do I get to meet this bloodsucker?"

"Michael," Brian sighs.

"How come you haven't introduced us yet?" He lowers his voice dramatically. "Was he in a terrible accident before being turned? Is he a horrifying, Phantom-of-the-Opera mess?"

"It hasn't been that long. I don't want you scaring him off."

"It's been a couple of months; you've never had a boyfriend for longer than that, so this one has to be special. You're glowing. I am nauseous. This means that it's time."

The logistics of Michael and Kyle in the same room make his head spin. He knows that Michael can be a little overwhelming; and besides, he isn't sure if Kyle has an interest in meeting his family just yet. It's a big step to take.

"Okay," he relents. "I'll ask him how he feels about it. But I'm not promising anything. If he's not on board, the answer is no."

He's dressed for work, sitting on the couch finishing a last-minute round of email replies with a granola bar hanging out of his mouth, when his phone buzzes with a text message from Kyle.

i'm passing by, you on your way to work already?

He replies: *nope, not yet*

can i come up? i'm outside

It's odd for Kyle to just show up like this, but he tells him to come up. Seeing him will put a smile on Brian's face for the rest of the night, and that's never a bad thing.

"It's open," he calls, when Kyle knocks.

Kyle shrugs off a light jacket as he crosses the room. He wears a tight pair of dark-wash jeans and a shirt with sleeves cut off mid-bicep. It's tight across the shoulders and hikes up enough to show skin when he flexes his arms above his head.

"Hey," he says, sliding down onto Brian's lap.

Brian can't stop gawking. Kyle's hair is gelled up into spikes. Between that and the new clothes, he looks ridiculously sexy.

"Hey, you," he replies, claiming a kiss. "Hot date?"

Kyle smirks. "I've been waiting to get you before work for *days*. You always look so cute in your scrubs." He goes right for neck kisses, then, his lips passing over the faded mark at the apex of Brian's neck and shoulder in a purposeful way. This is acknowledged as a sex button in their relationship, and Brian breathes out slowly, trying to control his reaction. It's unfair how easily Kyle can undo his resolve to maintain a strict schedule.

"I have work in an hour—"

"Mm," Kyle hums in reply, one hand between them, slowly rubbing him through his loose scrub pants. "I have been thinking about you all day." He lowers his voice even further, spreading the shape of Brian's thickening shaft between his fingers. "About touching you, making you come." The next kiss is bold, full of tongue and teeth. "Let me make you come."

"H-honey," he moans.

"I'll be quick," Kyle insists, sliding to his knees on the carpet. "I'll catch all the mess." His eyes sparkle with sultry intention, tongue out against his plump lower lip, fingers stroking up and down Brian's thighs. He's trembling, and seeing him this eager is too much for Brian to resist.

"Okay." He bites back a noise when Kyle leans over to nuzzle and kiss him through his pants. "Oh, *so* okay." He lets his head tip back, one hand finding its way into Kyle's hair.

It only occurs to him when Kyle lifts his cock out of the front of his boxers and over the waistband of his scrubs that they've never done this—it's always been the other way around. Brian has never really kept tabs on the give and take, because it doesn't matter to him what they do together so long as it's mutual and enjoyable; but Kyle's tongue and mouth that close bring him up short. He thinks he should say something, but he isn't sure what.

"Okay?" Kyle asks.

Sometimes it's impossible to hide things from your vampire boyfriend.

"First time," he says, stroking Kyle's jaw.

"Tell me if I do something wrong," Kyle says, and licks a broad stripe over the head of Brian's cock, ending the discussion.

"Oh, *god*."

A bead of fluid swells at his slit. Kyle licks it away.

Thankfully, there are no fangs involved. It's all wet licks and kisses in the beginning, Kyle exploring the tip and then the shaft, smearing saliva with his fingers and palm and then finally, finally his mouth closing around Brian. The sight and feel of those pale cheeks hollowing around his cock is enough to make Brian's fingers twist involuntarily in Kyle's hair.

Kyle starts bobbing, up and down, up and down, all tongue and jagged breathing in and out of his nose, and Brian loses it; his hips begin moving and his breathing goes off. Heat floods every inch of him, sweat prickles underneath his clothes, and it's hopeless to try to stay still inside that eager mouth.

"Feels good," he moans. "God, just like that. Use your hand, okay? Just like that, oh, god, yeah."

In the past, boyfriends have always stop-start blown him, to breathe or wipe their faces or to readjust, but Kyle just sucks and strokes in an endless loop of mouth and hand and Brian gets there a hell of a lot faster than he figured he would. "Y-you don't have to—I'm—"

And he just goes faster, and then—*faster*, his head an unnatural blur in Brian's lap. It's a little scary, but that doesn't stop Brian from coming suddenly in his mouth with a surprised cry.

He's still panting, tingling all over, when he asks, "Is that going to make you sick?"

Kyle laughs, his forehead on Brian's knee. "I guess we'll see? I don't think so, though. It's not enough to do anything."

There's come smeared across the corner of his mouth. Brian swipes at it with his thumb, only to have Kyle suck it between his lips when he starts to retreat. He withdraws it, Kyle's pursed mouth clinging to it the entire way.

He huffs out a breath. "God, that was—amazing, thank you."

"I'm so glad you feel that way, because then you won't be mad at me for making you late for work?" Kyle asks, chewing his lip.

"Oh, geez." Brian checks the time. He is going to be late, even if he gets in his car right now. "I'll text Erica. Don't worry about it."

Kyle tucks him back into his pants with an impish smile.

5

"I think you're going to want to see this," Clara says, handing him a Mansford, Illinois newspaper clipping.

It's a missing person bulletin on the police blotter from his hometown, and it's for him, but it's not calling him out as a criminal or saying that he's dangerous; all it says is that he's missing. It lists the day of his graduation as the last known date he was seen and gives a few details about his appearance and where to send information if anyone has seen him.

"Someone is looking for you," she says, sitting on the chair across from his bed. "I looked into it. I know I shouldn't have, but—you work for us, and I had to know what we might need to prepare for." She raises her eyebrows. "Turns out someone just misses you."

He's embarrassed. Upset too, but mostly embarrassed. "There are no charges, no warrant, nothing? You're sure?"

"No. And even if they were completely covering that up beyond my means to check to keep from scaring you deeper into hiding, they wouldn't bother to phrase it this way for the public or use this as the vehicle. They don't care about vampires' civil rights much; they'd arrest you and throw you behind bars if they thought you'd stolen a candy bar, not handle you with kid gloves like this." She shrugs. "The bulletin is weeks old and they're still running it statewide. Someone cares about you. And whatever you did, the police haven't figured it out yet." "But that doesn't mean they wouldn't, if they questioned me and put all the pieces together," he answers, shoving the grimy paper across the bed and putting his face in his hands.

He's tired. He hasn't seen Brian for a couple of days, and every time they go more than a day or so without being physically close he fills up with anxiety. His last customer was difficult. He's having dinner with Brian and his brother this weekend, and he wants to make a good impression—Michael is a huge part of Brian's life and Kyle knows how important it is to them both that Michael like him—but he has no idea how he can do that when his past is constantly lurking behind his thoughts, poisoning every gesture with dishonesty.

If Brian *knew*.

If Brian knew that he'd killed, that he'd run away from what he'd done, that Jeffrey—while guilty of his own trespasses—had parents and friends who probably still have no idea what happened to him and why, what would Brian think of him?

If Brian knew.

Brian, who cares about everyone. Who stops on the street to talk to homeless people and buys them coffee. Who treats every single vampire that comes through his center with the same respect and kindness, no matter how they treat him in return. Who can't go to the local animal shelter to rescue a dog or cat, because if he did he'd end up taking them all home—he could never leave one behind. Who donates to twelve different charities althoiugh he probably will be broke by the time he graduates; the money he inherited from his mother is just enough to cover living expenses and tuition. Who is the epitome of goodness, who sees the best in everyone, who gives out second and third and fourth chances like candy.

Would Brian still love him and want him, if he knew?

Clara sits next to him, head tilted. "You haven't told him."

Kyle bites his lip. Tears burn in his eyes, but he doesn't want to cry in front of her. "No." His voice is thick with self-loathing.

"You really love him," she says, sounding a little surprised.

"Do you think—" he shudders, curling his arms around himself. "Do you think that if I were older, if I had been a vampire longer, that I wouldn't love him as much?"

"I think that we disconnect from the things we want to disconnect from," she says. "We have the capacity to withdraw from trauma, from unpleasant things, from acts that warp humans irrevocably, but—we can love just as completely as they can, when we choose to.

The problem is, when it's a human we choose, it can be complicated." She frowns. "If you aren't careful, you can hurt him badly. And I don't mean just while feeding."

He stares at her, suddenly curious. "Did you...?"

She blinks, looking away. "There was another girl, when I was in high school. I—I haven't spoken to her since."

"I'm sorry," he says.

"It was for the best," she replies, recovering quickly. "I met Elisa because it didn't work out, and I'm happy here. I'm happy with her."

"I am, too," Kyle says, smiling, and puts a hand on her arm. "Happy here, that is. Thank you—I would never have looked into this on my own, and if something does happen at least I'll be prepared."

"Don't mention it," she says, from the doorway. "I mean that literally; don't mention it. I'd never hear the end of it."

He smiles, nodding.

✶

"Do you think this color is too much? I should've gone with basic black, I just—it felt like I was going to a funeral, and—"

Brian smiles and strokes the back of Kyle's neck. "You look great. Stop worrying. Michael and Jenn are going to love you."

Kyle paces, little blurs of supernatural speed at each turn of his heels. Brian worries about the integrity of his living room carpet; as if Kyle can read his mind, he shifts over onto the hardwood with an apologetic grimace.

"How do you know that? He's a lawyer and she's a veterinarian and I suck blood for a living," Kyle huffs, biting at his lip until it's bloody—it heals almost instantly, so he keeps doing it. "What are we going to talk about; what am I going to say? Oh, my god!"

Brian runs a lint roller over his jacket one last time and then takes Kyle's hands in his. "You're going to talk about how you came to Chicago to start a new life after high school." He kisses Kyle's knuckles, one by one. "You're going to talk about how you met a goofball with a disturbingly large comic book collection who seduced you with science. You're going to talk about how you have made that goofball very happy and how he hopes that you are as crazy about him as he is about you."

Kyle swallows thickly. "Brian, I—"

The buzzer for the downstairs door goes off, and Brian smiles. "Later?"

"Sure."

He hangs back as Michael and Jenn exchange hugs and small talk with Brian at the door, but it's not long before Brian guides them into the living room.

"Kyle, this is my brother Michael and his girlfriend, Jenn Chapelle. Michael, Jenn, this is my boyfriend, Kyle."

Michael gives Kyle a long, hard once-over, but then spoils the effect by sweeping him up into a back-clapping hug. "It's about damned time," he says, putting Kyle at arm's length again. "Does the lopsided physical-strength distribution negate the cradle robbing?"

Jenn puts a hand over her face and sighs. She's as tall and well-built as her better half; Brian laughs at the sight of Kyle dwarfed between them, a bewildered expression on his face.

He grumbles. "Michael." His brother knows very well that Kyle and Brian are only a few years apart in age, despite Kyle's outward appearance to the contrary.

"Oh, man, I am just messing with you," he says to Kyle, who looks as if he might prefer death to this moment. "Sorry, I had to. You're adorable. Come on, let's eat. I've got some donations stored up, brought them along. What's your poison?" He slings an arm around Kyle's shoulder.

"Um, B pos," Kyle replies, eyes still a little wide.

They sit at the table. Brian and Jenn chat quietly.

"I'll get our food," he says to her. "Michael, is the temperature okay or do you need me to warm it up?" Michael hands over a cooler bag filled with blood packets.

"Do you take it cold, Kyle?"

"Sometimes. Warm is fine tonight. Thanks," he says, smiling at Brian.

"Warm for me, too, then," Michael says.

Jenn follows Brian into the kitchen.

"That's a good sign, isn't it? He doesn't bother teasing if he doesn't approve," she says, helping Brian collect the food that's been warming in the oven.

Brian smiles and hugs her again, just because she deserves it for being the sister he never had. He's very grateful that they've all managed to clear an evening to get together. It would've been stilted if only Michael had been able to meet Kyle tonight; Jenn has become such an important member of their little family.

"He's been pacing all afternoon," Brian whispers. "He's really sensitive about himself. Sometimes I have a hard time talking about it with him, because the way I see him isn't the way he sees himself."

"You wear your heart on your sleeve." She balances the salad bowl and some utensils in her arms. "Him, not so much. Is it getting serious?"

Brian tastes the soup on the stove to make sure it's not undersalted. He frowns thoughtfully. "You know the funny part about that? It always has been. Serious, I mean. From the minute I met him. I don't know in what way exactly, but—it was never just casual. Never."

She grins, her short brown hair bobbing around her face. "Oh, god, you're done for."

"What?" he asks, smiling.

"Them's forever words," she says in a put-on Southern accent, eyebrows waggling.

"All right. Food. Dining room. You've teased me enough," he says, smiling even more brightly.

Brian is surprised to find Michael and Kyle engaged in rapid conversation. He and Jenn arrange the food, and Brian pours the blood and stirs in the anticoagulant. Michael takes his thoughtlessly, but Brian brings Kyle's to his side and sits down next to him, tangling their free hands.

"I had no idea you were involved in that case," Kyle is saying. "I followed it in the news for weeks. It was better than reality television, I swear."

"It was even better behind the scenes, and I will also say that the personal bets I collected on after it was over totally outweighed the actual compensation," Michael says, laughing. "Er, you know.

Friendly wagers, nothing of monetary value, of course."

"Of course," Kyle says, smiling, eyes bright with amusement.

Brian eats slowly, looking back and forth between them, and reality dawns.

They *like* each other.

He feels instantly and irrationally jealous. Michael didn't even like *him,* until he was twenty. He almost laughs, and shares a look with Jenn that says, *Well, so much for worrying about that.*

They discuss a variety of things as the evening passes—Michael's legal career, Jenn's animal hospital, Brian's time in the lab last semester, Kyle's search for a decent performing arts program that might accept a late admission; and then they come back around to lighter things, like the food and Brian's apartment, which leads to a question about living arrangements that makes both Brian and Kyle blush and stutter.

"And why not? With the cost of living in this city, it makes sense," Michael insists, setting down his glass and wiping blood from his lips.

Kyle's fingers twitch across Brian's knee under the table and Brian puts a hand on Kyle's thigh in return. The mutual touch calms him. "Kyle is settled where he is, and I'm hardly ever here, so for now it's fine. Right, honey?"

"Right," Kyle agrees, nodding.

Jenn strokes Michael's arm. "They're young. Stop meddling."

"Who's meddling? I am *guiding*. I'm an older brother; it's my duty."

"No, it's okay," Kyle says, surprising Brian. "Brian is lucky to have such a caring family. Speaking of that, how did you two meet?"

"Oh, god," Jenn sighs.

"Let me tell it," Michael says. She waves her hands in defeat.

"So, I had this case that required me to spend a lot of time with a client who had a *lust* for cats. I mean, it was off the charts. Blah blah blah lots of legal mumbo jumbo, what's important here is that this grand old broad fell in love with me. After I won the case for her, she insisted that I take one of her favorite cat's new kittens. She said it was meant to be. She named the little fuzzball after me. I couldn't say no, even though, let me tell you—I am *not* a cat person." He grins, waving his hands. "Shocker. So—I took it, and yes, I called it "It" because I just couldn't bring myself to call it 'Michael.' But It slowly grew on me."

"He'd like you to think that he didn't love that cat, but he *loved* that cat," Jenn interjects.

"Shh, dramatic flow, no interruptions," Michael chants. "So even though I refused to call it 'Michael' and kept calling it 'It,' okay, yes—I kind of liked It after a while. And then one night I found It vomiting blood, and I was devastated. Freaked out, called every animal hospital I could find and the only all-night facility was—"

"Mine," Jenn fills in, her bright green eyes lighting up with the memory.

"She stayed up with me and that cat all night," Michael says.

"He didn't make it," she says, frowning.

"Yeah. He was a tough little bugger, like his dad, but—there was nothing she could do."

"Oh," Kyle sighs, chin on his hands, his eyes wide. "Poor little guy."

"So there I am in my sweats, grief-stricken; I mean this was a *moment*, and—"

"I asked him out, like a total creeper," Jenn announces proudly.

"It was kind of creepy. 'Sorry about your cat, cuppa coffee?'"

"Oh my god, I was not that bad," she replies, swatting him. "You were just jumpy because you thought I hadn't figured out that you were a vampire, as if that mattered."

Brian watches Kyle watch them, and his heart aches with fondness. Kyle looks so touched by their romantic urban tale. "That's actually kind of sweet. I mean, the non-cat-dying parts, anyway," he says.

After the meal, Michael stands and starts clearing the table. "Give me a hand, Brian?"

They disappear into the kitchen together, leaving Jenn and Kyle to talk. Michael speeds through dish loading about ten times faster than he can, so Brian sits on the counter and watches him go at it.

He waits. He knows that he's about to get grilled about something; Michael always has something to say. He isn't at all surprised when his brother touches the collar of his shirt, then tugs the cloth aside with a single fingertip.

"He's feeding from you?" he asks.

There is still a mark on his skin (they do it too often for there not to be, now), and Brian's shirt isn't hiding it well to begin with. "Don't start."

"I want to make sure that you're okay," he replies. "I know that you probably know more about it than I do, but you can't blame me for worrying."

"We're safe, we're fine, it's fine," Brian says. He smiles, touching Michael's arm. "Thanks. But really, we know what we're doing." He blushes. Feeding doesn't have to be a sexual act, but Michael knows him too well—he doesn't do things by half, and intimacy is the only path by which he'd invite that sort of thing into his life.

"He doesn't talk about himself much," Michael observes.

"He's been through a lot," Brian says. "He's—kind of starting over."

"Just be careful, okay? I see the way you look at each other. When you care about someone like that, it's just as easy to hurt him as it is to make him happy."

Brian hugs his brother around the waist. "I'm going to do everything I can to make sure that doesn't happen."

✷

After Michael and Jenn leave, Kyle collapses onto the couch, his legs and arms all splayed in different directions. "I am such a kid," he declares, groaning. "I might as well have been drawing on the table with crayons the entire time while drinking blood from a sippy cup. What is it with your family and big amazing impressive *success*?"

Brian laughs, but not unkindly. Kyle looks so crestfallen. He sits on the couch and drags Kyle into his lap. "They adored you. They did. Trust me, you haven't seen them when they dislike someone. It's like the kitchen scene in *Jurassic Park*; two velociraptors, one on either side of you, and they are both starving."

Kyle laughs but then grows serious immediately and drops his face onto Brian's shoulder. "I want you to be proud of me when you introduce me to people who matter to you, but I don't see how you can be when I'm not proud of myself."

What to say to that? Brian wraps his arms around Kyle and settles on the first thing that comes to his mind. "I love you." Kyle stiffens. His eyes glaze over. "I love how strong and determined you are. I love that you feel so much. I love that things are sacred to you; you don't compromise. You're a fighter. And despite everything you've been through you're here, right now, sharing your life with me, and making me feel like the luckiest guy in the world."

"You don't know everything about me," Kyle confesses, sounding just as miserable as he is elated by Brian's declaration. "But I—I love you, too. I am so—so in love with you." Tears fall, despite his obvious effort to hold them back.

Brian kisses him, thumbing them away. "When you're ready to tell me more, I'm here, okay?"

Underneath it all, though, he's terrified. What hasn't Kyle told him?

✶

Kyle can be single-minded. When he wants and has permission to act on that want, he has an issue with stopping. This, he has learned, can happen when you go from a life of denial into the arms of a man who gives you everything and makes you feel safe and desired.

At times he thinks that Brian is about to stop him, to say "you don't have to," or "let's do something else," or "let me take care of you," but then there he is, in his adorable scrub top with his brown skin and his bright eyes and his neck that—all biting jokes aside—is begging to be kissed every minute of every day. There he is, with his reading glasses and textbooks and tired little feet. There he is, blushing and losing his breath every time Kyle comes near. There he is, full of blood that tastes so sweet. And he's all Kyle's.

"Baby," Brian gasps. Kyle has pushed him down onto the arm of the couch before he's even had time to kick off his shoes, coming back home from the movies; and now his pants are open and Kyle is on his knees on the carpet with a full mouth. "Stop, stop, stop."

Kyle pulls off wetly, licking his swollen lips. "Sorry, yes?"

"I love your mouth on me, but can I do something for you?" he asks, panting.

Kyle blushes. He knows what he wants, but he's not comfortable with the language. "Um. If I—can I do something that will lead to you doing something for me?" He thumbs Brian's belly, unable to stop his eyes from drifting over Brian's trim waist and muscular legs. He can hear Brian's heartbeat thumping faster and smell the blood rushing through his veins.

"What did you have in mind?"

"I want to, um, explore a little more?"

He trails his fingers down along the curve of Brian's ass, hoping that the message is clear enough. He can't bring himself to say those words just yet. He tries, but they feel so crude. Brian blushes and sucks in his bottom lip. He looks almost shy for a moment, his hands tightening around the arm of the couch, his throat bobbing with a reflexive swallow.

Kyle kisses the flat of his hip. "Only if you want to."

"Could we—" He strokes the back of Kyle's neck. "Bed, first?"

Kyle is relieved. He'd thought that Brian might suggest a shower, and he does not want to taste soap right now. He can smell Brian, the musk of his body and of his arousal. Neither are offensive, only natural and human and masculine, and Kyle wants to taste them rather badly.

He stops Brian at the foot of the bed and begins to undress him. The tie goes first, loosened with careful motions, then the vest and the shirt beneath it. Brian's strong shoulders practically beg for kisses as they're revealed. He huffs out a harsh breath and clasps Kyle around the waist. Just as eager for attention are Brian's chest and ribs and belly, which go rough with goosebumps when Kyle kisses and licks them. Kyle nudges Brian to sit on the bed and they crawl toward the center together, his mouth dragging damply down Brian's belly as Brian shimmies out of the rest of his clothes.

"All day," Brian groans, messing Kyle's hair with his hands as Kyle's mouth travels down and inward, finding the softer hair at his inner thigh. "Thought about this all day."

Kyle can't claim innocence; they'd ended their usual date day at the movies and Kyle had left his hand on Brian the entire time, on his knee or thigh or around his shoulders, and there had been moments when he'd snuggled close and buried his face in Brian's neck. He hadn't done anything sexual, but he hadn't given Brian any space or hope of retreat, either.

He licks eagerly over Brian's cock, pressing the backs of his thighs until they lift, exposing him more completely. He nuzzles down to the base of Brian's shaft, and then licks at his balls with long, wet drags of the flat of his tongue. He tastes so good. He feels even better.

They haven't discussed going further.

Kyle can sense Brian's hesitation both naturally and supernaturally; he understands it, but he wants to make Brian feel good more than anything else. He wants to touch and taste. He wants to feel Brian come apart around him. He can't explain it—no one has done these things to him, so how can he want so much to do them to someone else?

To give them a moment, he rises on his knees and sheds his clothing slowly, piece by piece, watching Brian watch him. He drops his eyes only when Brian's gaze settles on the bulge tenting his briefs.

Brian makes him feel so sexy. Powerful. Confident. The way his eyes go wet and wanting every time Kyle initiates, every time Kyle pushes for something new—

Kyle tugs behind Brian's knees, encouraging them upward again, exposing Brian's ass to the air. He kisses one upturned knee. He kisses down the inside of Brian's thigh, stroking his balls with one hand and then lifting them up and out of the way.

"Oh my god," Brian whimpers.

Kyle's voice is almost a growl when he asks, "Can smell you, you're so—have to taste you—can I put my mouth down there, please?"

"Oh, god, yes, yeah." Brian's hands flutter. "There's—stuff, bedside drawer."

Kyle blurs to get there and back almost instantly. He doesn't want to waste a second. He doesn't want to think too much about the lubricant and condoms just yet, though he knows he'll be glad when the time comes that he stopped to gather the necessities sooner rather than later. First, though, he wants to take his time.

Brian looks so wanton spread out on the bed, his body a compact human buffet Kyle wants to sample in as many ways as he can. He presses wet kisses down the back of one thigh and then all the way up to his prize, which he greets with a brush of his fingertips. He presses his lips to the skin beneath Brian's balls. He has no clue what he's doing, but there are only a few things to do, he supposes, and all of them are things that he desperately wants to do right now.

Brian pants, scrubbing his fingers through Kyle's hair. "Please," he gasps, twisting. "Please, please, more. Want you there so bad."

The way he *smells*. It's not even just clean sweat and Brian smell and sex smell—it's the way all those scents combine that makes Kyle's body throb. It makes him think this will never be enough, that having Brian over and over again will never be enough. A lifetime won't be enough. A vampire's lifetime wouldn't be enough.

He spreads Brian's cheeks apart and licks across his hole, kisses it wetly. God, the way he tastes. Salty and tangy and—

"Oh," Brian moans. His whole body trembles and the muscles in his thighs are taut.

Kyle dives in again, sucking kisses into the wrinkled rim. Brian's taste is so concentrated here, sharp and earthy, and Kyle's mouth floods with saliva. He wants more. His cock throbs against the bed so insistently that he has to tear his attention away from the sensation or risk coming from the friction alone. This becomes a simpler task when Brian starts to babble and thrust down against his tongue.

"Inside," he whimpers, after a long round of slow, wet licking. "Inside me, inside me, okay? Oh, oh god—"

"Taste so good," Kyle groans, holding Brian open.

It's trickier than he thought, breaching that ring of muscle smoothly. He has to be careful; if he applies too much force he could hurt Brian. This worry doesn't stop him licking in until half his tongue is buried inside of the hot, clenching space.

Where an average human might have trouble with a cramping tongue or jaw while doing this, Kyle doesn't, and so it's easy to settle into a rhythm, using his chin to set the angle while thrusting his tongue in and out, in and out, his thumbs stroking the sensitive skin around the rim while his fingers keep Brian's cheeks apart.

Brian is a mess in record time, reduced to gasps and whines long before Kyle has his fill, his pelvis writhing desperately in search of better friction. Kyle comes up for air only when there's so much spit and Brian is so loose that he's sure any more of this will just push him into useless oversensitivity.

"God," Brian breathes, staring down at him, red-faced and sweating. "I—I've never—no one has ever—not like *that*, I mean, oh, my god."

Kyle grins at him, feeling eager and accomplished. "More?"

"Fingers," Brian pants. "Lube and fingers, please. If you are okay with that."

"Okay" is an understatement.

He squeezes out a handful of cool lubricant, his heart pounding. It's messy and unfamiliar (he'd just used hand lotion when he masturbated back at home, and then only on the rare occasions when he'd wanted to take his time). "Would it be, um, easier, on your stomach?"

Brian exhales noisily as the pad of Kyle's lubricant-slick thumb begins rubbing slow circles around his hole. "M-maybe, but—I want—" He stops, mouth dropping open at a particularly well-aimed stroke. "Want to watch."

Kyle shivers. "Oh."

He trades his thumb for his middle finger and goes from rubbing to pressing and then, after a moment has passed, to sinking wetly inside, knuckle by knuckle, turning the digit and crooking it—doing so feels natural—until it's in as far as it can go.

"Oh," Brian whimpers. "Up. Up, sort of—up and in."

He doesn't say anything, just corrects his angle and starts over. He's nervous. He doesn't want to hurt Brian and he doesn't want to do this the wrong way.

Brian pants and shifts around a little, but otherwise says nothing as Kyle begins working his finger in and out, in and out. Kyle isn't exactly sure what he's looking for, or what reaction he's waiting for, but he'll keep going until Brian tells him otherwise. He finds it with two fingertips as he slides them back—Brian gasps and tenses.

"Th-there?" he asks. He doesn't even know what he's touched, but it is firm where most of what's inside of Brian's ass feels soft and smooth.

"Shorter presses, just—" He finds it again, and Brian jerks. "Oh!"

"Whoa," Kyle breathes, watching Brian's cock jump and spit a bead of fluid.

"You figured that out way faster than I thought you would," Brian moans, sounding wrecked. "I'm not going to last very long if you keep doing that."

Kyle changes his angle, presses deeper and lower. "I can avoid it," he says roughly. "I can—do this instead."

"God, honey." Brian clenches greedily around his finger.

He speeds up again, listening to the wet suck of Brian's body trying to keep his fingers inside. It's so hot, the way his ass *clings*.

"Another?"

"No," Brian answers, licking spit from the corner of his mouth. "Want you. Want you inside of me."

He crawls up Brian's body and settles over him, chest to chest, pelvis to pelvis and shuddering at the warmth; they both radiate heat. Brian's mouth is like a gift after so much time spent alone down there between his legs, and it all seems to just come together, Brian's limbs around him and their bodies and mouths slotted together perfectly. He loves being this close to Brian, loves the way Brian's face shows everything he's feeling, his emotions so raw and readable.

"Love you," he whispers, thumbing Brian's swollen mouth. "Love you, love you so much."

Brian pushes Kyle's underwear off, and Kyle shivers as his cock rises against his belly.

"God, I love you, too." Brian kisses his neck and searches between their bodies, finding Kyle's cock aching and hard. Kyle hisses. Brian whispers, stroking him, "Want this inside. Okay?" His other hand squeezes Kyle's ass, guides Kyle's pelvis between his thighs.

"Yes," Kyle whimpers, thrusting through the circle of his fist. "I—I'm ready."

Brian fumbles with the condom. Putting it on is inelegant and embarrassing, but that's Brian's hand rolling the latex down, Brian's hand squeezing him, stroking him, slicking him up and guiding him without breaking eye contact. He takes over once he's trapped between these plush cheeks, the head of his cock wedged snugly against Brian's spit-softened rim. He rolls his hips and presses forward, and this part too isn't as smooth as he'd expected; he wriggles a bit too much for his own liking, but finally Brian's body gives way and he sinks clumsily into the tightest, hottest sheath he has ever felt.

"Oh," he whimpers, grasping Brian's jaw. "Oh, *god*."

"Come on," Brian answers, movement steeling his back as he rocks, lifting his ass into the thrust. "Come on, I'm—I'm so stretched, you won't hurt me."

That Kyle doesn't have to stop for rest works toward concealing the fact that he has never done this before and has no idea what he's doing. He can simply do whatever Brian asks for, faster or harder or slower or at a change of angle, while focusing on kissing the trembling mouth below his and on not coming every time Brian's ass drags around the shaft of his cock like a fist with a heartbeat and a heat source all its own.

More than anything, he wants to remember Brian's face as it looks right now. He wants to be able to look back someday and recall the way his eyelids flutter, the way his mouth has fallen open, the way his eyes glitter as he chases his own pleasure.

And somewhere in the middle he realizes that, despite how roughly he plunges in and out of Brian, despite how Brian twists and sobs under him every time he comes down just right, their eyes never stray far from each other's faces and they're both thinking the same thing.

They're together, moving as one.

These are Brian's fingernails scratching red marks down his back, Brian's heels digging into his hips. This is Brian's impossibly tight ass pulsing around his cock, Brian's human sweat smell tracked all over them both as if it's in the air as well as on their skin. This is Brian's pulse racing and the smell of his blood rushing, rushing, rushing through his veins.

All at once, Kyle wants to bite. He wants to bite so badly, just a shallow bite, just a few sips, just enough to feel the backlash of Brian's pain and pleasure through the blood, he wants—he *knows* that it will bring them closer together, that it will complete this act in a way no mere orgasm ever could.

He blinks hazily into Brian's lust-blown pupils, hips snapping back and forth. "Brian—"

"Do it," Brian answers, touching the tips of their noses together. "My shoulder, do it on my shoulder."

Kyle almost loses it then and there and has to stop thrusting to back off. "O-oh, god." He breathes frantically. He's never lasted this long, never even tried to.

He licks over a soft spot on Brian's shoulder and finds what he's looking for; it only takes a moment to encourage his fangs to come down and by then Brian is whimpering for them, staring at them and licking his lips and rocking around Kyle's cock.

"Please, now, now, okay, just—need you to, need to feel you, need you to make it *hurt*, please—"

"Just breathe, okay? Just—I'm here, I'm going to, I—"

When he bites down, Brian bucks up against him with a cry. He holds Brian down by his arms, letting go only when he retracts his teeth and begins to drink. It's a shallow, superficial break, only allowing for a few swallows before the coagulant begins to kick in, but that's okay. Brian is already overwhelmed and Kyle doesn't want him senseless right now.

He reaches between them, slowing his thrusts so he can focus on swallowing blood and stroking Brian's cock at the same time. He's reeling; the intimacy of the drinking combined with Brian's body's reaction is like an echo, Brian's pleasure right there in front of him, Brian's pleasure singing through his blood—it's almost too much. He is already so close.

"Don't stop. I'm going to come," Brian sobs, rutting up into Kyle's hand and then back down around his cock, over and over. "I'm going to, I can't—don't stop—*Kyle*—"

Kyle pulls off of Brian's shoulder, staring only briefly at the blood that drips sluggishly from the punctures. He wants to see Brian's face when he comes. He thrusts harder, deeper, letting Brian grind down against him, but mostly he focuses on working Brian's cock.

Brian's eyes roll back. His whole body tenses at once; his muscles cord up and stand out everywhere, and then he jerks in Kyle's hand and spurts, again and again, panting raspingly with every pulse.

Kyle reattaches himself to the bite marks and sucks. He can't resist; the smell is driving him crazy, Brian's pleasure-anguished face is burned on the inside of his eyelids, and he just wants to keep going. Brian throbs in his fist, crying out his name. Kyle swivels his hips—so *tight*, oh god—and keeps licking at the bite, and Brian's cock continues to dribble wetness, weaker and weaker until he's just shuddering.

The bleeding has stopped. Kyle pulls away, mouth stained, fangs sinking back into his gums. He's still dizzy and he hasn't even come. Brian kisses across his lips and he twitches away—his mouth is covered in blood—but Brian's tongue is there, undeterred, licking his own blood off of Kyle's mouth.

"You don't have to—"

Brian's voice is wrecked. "I like it," he rasps, sounding guilty. "I like—I like the way it hurts, I like the way it looks, I like the way it tastes. I—is that wrong, I—"

"No, god, no, not at all, I," Kyle pants, trying to focus. He needs to come so badly his balls ache, but if he moves he's going to spill placidly into the condom and he doesn't want it to be an afterthought like that.

Brian is still trembling. He nudges their faces together and curls his pelvis upward, slow and careful, drawing the tight clench of his body around Kyle's pulsing cock.

"Close," Kyle whines.

"I can't believe you're still hard," Brian says, their mouths brushing. "Feels so good."

"If I so much as breathe too fast I'm going to, um, instantly," Kyle says, so on edge that even talking about it doesn't help.

The warmth from Brian's skin and breath ghosts intimately over Kyle's face. His voice is so low, so husky when he says, "It's okay." He licks across Kyle's lips and then inside, kissing him, filling his mouth with tongue. "Come inside of me, sweetheart." His fingers squeeze Kyle's ass, pull him in deeper. "Want you to."

"Oh, god," Kyle whispers, pushing as deeply as he can go; it takes three grinding thrusts for him to fall apart, groaning into the sweaty curve of Brian's wounded shoulder, the smell of the blood pushing him over even faster. They kiss, sweet and lazy, pant into each other's mouths and grin like idiots for what feels like ages.

Brian helps him get rid of the condom, and after they roll over onto the dry side of the bed they collapse into each other's arms.

"Your shoulder," he says sleepily. "Do you have first aid stuff?"

"Same drawer," Brian says. His weary head is already on the pillow, his hair a sweaty mess, his mouth curled into a satiated smile.

Kyle smiles too, through cleaning and bandaging the bite marks. He ducks his face against Brian's chest when it's finished wanting to be close, to share every last second of this blissful, throbbing, damp aftermath.

"Hey," Brian breathes, eyelids dipping. "I see you hiding that smile. That is against the rule."

"The no-hiding-smiles rule?"

"Yep, that one."

Kyle props his chin on Brian's chest. "Noted." He brushes wavy, damp strands of hair off Brian's forehead. "Did you—did you want to do that the other way around the first time? I—I know we didn't talk about it much."

"Whatever vague idea I had," Brian says, "yours was much better."

Kyle bites his lip. "Okay." He grins. He laughs, when that isn't enough, joy bubbling up in his chest.

Brian's fingers are restless, touching Kyle's bare skin everywhere they can reach. "You were wonderful." He rolls them over and reaches for the covers. "Stay the night?"

Kyle sinks into his arms, too content and wiped out to answer.

6

Janice bends to pluck another grape from the bowl on Kyle's bedside table. Kyle leans with her so that the highlight foils in her dark hair aren't disturbed by the movement.

He lowers his voice, grinning shyly. "So, he had one of his textbooks open on the table while we ate—I mean, while he ate—which is totally normal. But he kept looking at me between pages. He's not usually so distracted when he's working, so I thought maybe he'd be interested in, you know, blowing it off a little—"

"Kyle," Janice breathes, scandalized.

"Can you blame me? You've met him. He's—" Kyle blushes, fanning himself with his gloved hands.

"The very definition of hotness. I know. Go on."

"He starts talking about bones, skeletal structure, all that. And then he asks me, 'Do you know how many bones there are in the human body?' And I say 'Yes, but I don't know them all by name or like, exactly which is where.' And he says, 'I'd be happy to teach you.'"

"Let me guess: he didn't mean out of the textbook?"

"Oh, god, did he ever *not* mean out of the textbook," Kyle answers, his face glowing bright red. "It took hours. By the end I don't think I even remembered my own name."

"Damn," she replies, while he fusses with her hair. "All the good ones are taken." She smiles playfully, her brown, full cheeks dimpling. "Or play for the other team."

"Oh, shut up," he replies, smiling. "Andrew is crazy about you and he is most definitely not gay. Despite the hair." He makes a face. "Let's also go ahead and forget about my clearly nonfunctional gaydar.

Man, that was an awkward conversation."

"Hush. He didn't care. And sure, we'd be good together, I think. If we could ever figure out what we both want," she sighs. "At least I know he's ready for this jelly."

"You will," Kyle insists, with a fond glance at her curvy figure. "And he totally is."

His phone rings. It takes him a second to remove the messy glove from his right hand and put it to his ear. It's Brian.

"Hey," he answers.

"Hey," Brian replies, and Kyle knows just by the tension in his tone that something is wrong. "I hate to cancel this early, but I don't think I'm going to be able to make dinner tonight." ("Dinner" is an hour they usually spend together around midnight in the parking lot of the blood center, making out like teenagers in the backseat of Brian's car.)

"Aw, what's up?" he asks, while Janice listens.

"There was a break-in at the center," Brian says. "We're going to be on and off with the police all day; they want to shut us down for investigation. We have to reroute all the vampires to the uptown center; it's going to be a complete mess. I won't be able to take a break. Might not even be able to answer my phone or texts."

Panic flashes through Kyle's body like a slap. "Um. Was anything stolen, or...?"

"I, uh, I can't say, sorry, it's—protocol."

"That's okay," he replies. "Just—drop me a text when you can? So I know you're okay."

"I will," Brian says, sounding more like himself. "I love you."

"I love you, too," he answers, and hangs up.

"Everything okay?" Janice asks.

"I think so," he lies, and dread rolls through him in waves.

It's twelve hours before Kyle hears from Brian again, and then only to receive the news that he's going to catch a few hours of sleep on a cot in the back room of the center before he gets right back to work.

Support staff is being flown in, but it may take another full day to get them up to speed, and Erica needs Brian.

It's three days before Brian is allowed to go home.

Kyle spends those three days taking extra clients and panicking. The surplus of human blood winds him up in ways that probably aren't good for the situation; when he takes in too much blood he feels things too keenly, and since his primary emotion at the moment is fear—

He asks Clara to look into the incident at the center.

"Aware of it already," she says. "They contacted us requesting that we donate to the uptown center instead."

"We donate to them on a regular basis?" Kyle asks.

"Yes," she answers. "How do you think Elisa found out about your boyfriend so quickly?" She smiles playfully. "They didn't volunteer specifics, of course. Just asked us to reroute due to the facility being 'closed for maintenance'. I poked around a little after I got off the phone; the rep who called was our normal contact but it seemed odd to me, the way he phrased the request."

"Is he local? Would he have firsthand information?"

"No, all the official back and forth is at the corporate level. They're based out of Dallas. But—like I was saying, it felt weird."

"And?" he urges, biting the inside of his cheek until it bleeds.

"Single intruder, male, a vampire judging by the way he tore the place up. No other description. I don't think they know anything yet, to be honest."

"Blood stolen?" he asks, his thoughts whirling a hundred miles an hour.

That would make sense. It happens all the time, vampires trying to break into blood centers by brute force; the attempts are rarely successful because it's typically the younger, more desperate ones who attempt it and they aren't smart or strong enough to get past security.

Please let it be that, he thinks.

"No," Clara replies, sounding suspicious. "That's the interesting part. No blood was stolen or consumed. The vampire went for the computers and presumably didn't find what he wanted, because after that he searched and destroyed the hard copy records room."

Fuck.

Clara reads his expression like an open book. "Are you trying to tell me that this has something to do with you, kid? If you know something, 'fess up now."

"N-no, I—no." He stares off into space, thinking of Brian's safety. It's the only thing that matters to him right now. "I don't want it to be about me. But I can't tell you for sure that it isn't."

She sighs. "I'll keep digging."

"On my way home soon," Brian says.

His voice is barely a whisper, and Kyle worries. "I'm coming over," he replies.

"I'm just going to sleep. Don't worry about me, honey. I'll call you in the morning."

Kyle holds his breath for a long, wounded moment. They haven't seen each other in days. Does Brian like to be alone when he's exhausted, or does he really not want to see Kyle?

"Let me take care of you," Kyle says. He can't remember ever wanting to do this for anyone but himself, before Brian; the urge both surprises and warms him. "You take care of me all the time, you take care of *everyone*, please let me—"

"I'm sorry. I want you there, I do." Brian's voice softens. "I've missed you so much."

Kyle gets to Brian's apartment before Brian does, but not before stopping to pick up some groceries on the way. He lets himself in with the spare keys Brian lent him, has the groceries put away in seconds and then thinks about what else he can do before Brian arrives. He sets out a clean towel and a fresh razor in case Brian wants to shower and shave. He takes out a pair of pajamas and Brian's favorite underwear. He waters Brian's plants and sets the mail neatly in the mail tray on his desk.

Out of ideas, he strips to his briefs and crawls into Brian's bed. He doesn't want Brian to think of entertaining him or feeding him or anything, so maybe he'll go to sleep before Brian gets home.

He's halfway there when the door opens; his ears perk up at the sound of steps but relax when he catches Brian's scent. He doesn't move, content to lie still as he listens to Brian lock the door, cross the apartment, come into the bedroom, kick off his shoes, shrug out of his jacket and trail sleepily toward the bed. It's a testament to his exhaustion that he doesn't stop to throw his clothes into the hamper, just wiggles out of each piece and lets it lie where it falls.

Kyle watches, eyes wide to combat the darkness of the bedroom, as Brian's naked form takes shape between the shadows.

Brian breathes, "Hey, you."

"Shh," Kyle replies, kneeling at the end of the bed and helping Brian into the clean underwear. "Come to bed."

Brian crawls into his arms and falls asleep before his head settles on the pillow.

Kyle wakes up early the next morning. He's halfway through fixing Brian's favorite granola-yogurt-fruit combination when Brian shuffles into the kitchen and wraps two arms around his waist from behind. He presses his face to the back of Kyle's neck and snuffles, pulling Kyle back against his body. Kyle relaxes into him.

It would be so easy to get used to this, he thinks.

"Orange or apple-cranberry?" he asks. "I bought both."

"Come back to bed," Brian murmurs huskily, kissing down the nape of Kyle's neck.

"Breakfast," he insists, though his stomach dips.

Brian's right hand splays across his belly and slides into his underwear, cupping him. "Come back to bed," he repeats, grinding a morning erection that couldn't be more obvious against Kyle's ass.

"Oh," he breathes.

It's been a nightmare of a week. Brian feels well and truly run through the mill. Thousands of details buzz inside his skull like angry flies. He's talked to so many law enforcement officers and federal blood distribution managers that he would be quite happy to never speak again, which is a first for him. His schedule and the rest of his summer at the center have been tossed up in the air, and he's not looking forward to the panic he knows he'll feel when it hits home just how much of his life must be reordered.

But for now—at least, for the next day or two—he doesn't have to think about any of it. Erica had shoved him out of her and John's apartment, telling him in no uncertain terms that if she heard from him before Monday she would personally have his business phone turned off. For perhaps the first time, she won't have to worry about carrying out that threat.

The moment Brian has Kyle back in bed, he doesn't want to think about anything but losing himself in every inch of his beautiful boyfriend. He's missed Kyle so much. This separation has left him empty and aching, and the promise of comfort in Kyle's arms is the light at the end of a very long and trying tunnel.

After they undress, he rolls Kyle beneath him and kisses him until they are both breathing heavily. Kyle smiles up at him, and Brian feels his face heat up as he licks his way into first one dimple and then the other, ending with a deep kiss that sends his tongue past Kyle's lips.

He loves that Kyle is slender, and longer than he is. He loves that Kyle is paler than he is, loves the freckles that dot his overall perfection like drops of bittersweet chocolate in vanilla ice cream. He loves the way that Kyle's limbs twine around him when they're like this, how he holds him close and takes him, just for a little while, out of the whirlwind that his life has become.

Kyle gasps when he sucks a nipple between his lips. "Oh."

"Missed you so much," he murmurs, tracing freckle after freckle across Kyle's ribs. Kyle arches higher into him the lower he goes, so that by the time he's nipping his way across a hip bone, his ass is off the bed.

"Please," he whimpers.

Brian lowers his mouth hungrily around Kyle's cock, sucking it hard and fast with no hint of a tease. Kyle is fully hard and when Brian pulls off to breathe he pushes up, desperate for more.

Brian smiles, licking his way down the swollen, vein-ribbed shaft. "Missed me too?"

"You have no idea," Kyle says. "Don't stop."

He doesn't want to stop making Kyle feel good, but he doesn't want to stop looking at him, either; drinking in Kyle's body with his eyes is one of his favorite things. He loves mapping the beautiful dips and lines of Kyle's forever-youthful body, loves the spots where he is still soft as much as the places where he had begun to lengthen and grow masculine-hard.

Kyle slides a bare leg around his torso and he bends lower, scattering kisses across his thighs. He nibbles all the way down to Kyle's knees and licks at the sensitive spots behind the joints, recalling with pleasure the afternoon he'd spent counting every bone in Kyle's body with his lips and tongue. He smiles, looking up at Kyle, and it's obvious that they are both thinking the same thing.

"I'm happy to repeat the lesson if it's slipped your mind," he says, dragging his tongue down Kyle's calf. He traces Kyle's ankle with his lips, and the upper arch of his foot, and then finds the space between his big toe and the smaller one just next to it.

Kyle inhales sharply, his eyes going dark. "I remember it very well," he forces out, his hips churning. His cock stands over his belly, bobbing eagerly. "Can—" He stops, licking his lips.

Brian gives him time, kisses back up to his neck and then on to his ear, letting their bodies line up again. "Mm?" He kisses Kyle's mouth, thrilling at the instant connection that snaps to life between them when their lips meet.

Kyle's other leg curls around him, drawing his pelvis up higher. "Can we—" His cheeks go pink. "All—all the way?"

Brian chest twinges with affection at how shy Kyle still is about verbalizing. He retrieves the lubricant and a strip of condoms from the bedside table. "Want to try a different position than last time?" He sits up, straddling Kyle's hips. This is obviously not what his boyfriend has in mind. His face remains that same, wanting shade of blushing pink. He looks eager and overwhelmed and Brian's heart skips a beat. Kyle's fingers slide along Brian's pelvis and continue downward, wrapping around Brian's erection. He squeezes and pulls. His thumb traces the swollen, still-dry head.

"Can we, um, switch?" he asks, his eyelashes fanned out across his red cheeks.

Oh, *god.*

"Yeah," Brian breathes, closing his eyes when Kyle's fist begins moving around him; the idea socks him in the gut and spreads though him, warm and almost too much. "Of course."

With an unexpected blur of supernatural movement Kyle flips them, straddles Brian's thighs, and smiles like a kid in a candy store as he pins Brian beneath him. "Really? It's okay?"

"So okay," Brian replies, half in awe and half turned on. He curls his hands around Kyle's slender waist, breathing in surprise when Kyle guides his hands lower, along the divide between his cheeks. The way that his round, perky ass swells up toward the dip of his lower back is sinfully perfect, and Brian can't help but trace and squeeze the shape with his fingers.

After a bit of rubbing and pressing, Brian slicks his fingers while Kyle gets comfortable over his pelvis, watching him with bright eyes. He's nervous, and his cock is throbbing.

"Touch me," he whines, when Brian's fingers don't go where he wants them to go fast enough. "Touch me there." His pelvis squirms, and Brian tries not to overreact—the slow twist of his pale body is unbearably erotic, as is the red blush that spills down his neck and chest and curls around the tips of his ears as he asks for Brian's fingers.

"I don't want to rush," Brian replies, stroking slippery fingers up and down the space between Kyle's cheeks, rubbing across his hole and the warm, hairy skin there, loving the way he feels.

"I waited," Kyle answers, head falling back in pleasure. "Was going to try this by myself, but I wanted you to be the first."

Brian aches at that, but he keeps stroking. He's nervous—he's never been anyone's first before, and even though he knows it's silly to think of this as the pinnacle of their sexual introduction (he firmly believes that penetration does not have to be the pinnacle of sex), it's still important to him to make it as good as it can be. He wants to do justice to the expectation on Kyle's face. He wants Kyle to recall the first time he let someone inside of his body with a smile and a blush, even if things between them don't work out in the long run.

He waits for Kyle to relax and slowly rubs circles around the rim of his hole. When he feels Kyle sit down harder on his fingers, he presses inward. "Breathe out and push against my finger," he says, and Kyle's hands flutter, one settling on his chest and the other fisting air uselessly as Brian's pointer finger slides inside of him.

"Oh," he moans, going still. "Oh, that feels weird."

"It will. Just relax, honey. Let yourself get used to it, it's okay."

"*Oh*."

Brian crooks the digit, lining up a second just for leverage's sake. "That's it. There you go. So beautiful for me."

A blush goes wild over his milky flesh again, darkening and spreading. Goosebumps spring up along his arms, and the hair there stands on end. He goes still, sitting back on his calves. His body does unwind considerably then, air filling his lungs as he gives over to the intrusion. His ass goes soft and spreads around Brian's fingers.

Brian's finger begins to move smoothly, working him open. A second finger is incorporated the same way, only this time Kyle's pelvis swivels to work against it. By the third finger he must begin to feel the burn, because he slows down and begins to pant, biting and licking his lips. Brian enjoys watching the muscles in his arms and shoulders and belly and thighs flicker and flex as he rocks back and forth, his pretty face scrunched up.

After a long, slick, tense while he twitches, his fingers spasming outward. He whines, digging his fingernails into Brian's belly. "Oh my god," he moans, hips moving. "Oh my *god*—"

Grinning, Brian crooks his fingers and begins moving them faster, in and out. Kyle's cock pulses and dribbles a few droplets of fluid onto Brian's stomach, and Brian has to bite down on his lip to stifle the whimper rising in his throat at the sight. He doesn't realize just how much it affects him to watch Kyle take his fingers until he speaks and his voice is threadbare. "Can we...?" He fumbles for the condom with his free hand, panting. "Are you comfortable there, or do you want to be somewhere else?"

"No, I want it like this," Kyle replies, staring down at him hungrily.

God.

Kyle shifts forward, letting Brian's fingers go with a grunt so that he can apply more lubricant. Brian's pulse stutters in response as he adjusts his pelvis to bring them into better alignment and Kyle is there all at once, the firm globes of his ass parting like warm silk, letting Brian push up between them.

"Please," he gasps. "Please, I want it." He reaches behind and under himself and guides Brian's cock, lining up its blunt head with his slick pucker. The head pops in easily—they both huff audibly at the sensation—but the shaft takes longer, overheated, frantic moments, Kyle's chest hitching as he sits down.

"Okay?" Brian asks, voice rough.

"D-don't move yet." He's sweating and shaking.

"Never, not until you're ready." Brian's fingers clutch Kyle's hips. The pressure around his cock is almost unbearable. Not all the tension in Kyle's body is positive, and the last thing Brian wants to do is hurt him.

It begins slowly, with small twitches of Kyle's pelvis, just enough movement to drag Brian's cock along his insides and make both their pulses stutter. Brian maintains a stranglehold on Kyle's hips as Kyle begins lightly moving up and down. He's as tight as a fist and twice as hot.

"God," Brian moans.

"So full," he whimpers.

"Don't wanna hurt you." His fingers slip in the sweat gathering on Kyle's skin.

"You aren't. It's just a lot."

Brian squirts more lubricant into his hand and then wraps it around Kyle's half-mast erection: nothing like a good distraction. He detours to drizzle more where the base of his cock is stretching Kyle open, then puts his hand back on Kyle's cock and strokes it slowly.

"Feels good," Kyle says.

"Have all the time in the world. No rush. Love touching you, honey."

They begin to move together gradually, Brian's stomach muscles burning as they relearn the particular sting that results from making his body churn up into another's. It's been a while.

Kyle begins to move at his own pace, pelvis churning forward and back, forward and back, his muscles flexing, his face twisting up. "Better," he moans, pushing his cock in and out of the circle of

Brian's fist. "Much better."

The wet noises of their bodies joining send arousal rushing through him, and as they grow louder and come faster, Brian's pleasure winds itself up tighter and tighter. Kyle's right hand fumbles for Brian's left and, though it's awkward, they tangle their fingers in mid-air.

Kyle whines, riding Brian's thrusts. "I'm okay, I'm fine, just keep doing that, keep—"

It's messy and off-rhythm the entire time, but it gets them there; and Kyle seems to enjoy being in control, while Brian is more than happy to surrender. Kyle begins climbing that edge, fucking between Brian's cock and hand, his face beet red and his fingers almost hurting Brian's, they are closed so tightly around them.

"Close," he spits, shaking, and Brian can see that his balls are drawn up and his slit is winking and wet, bisecting a swollen cock head. "Close—oh, god, *oh*—I'm gonna come." He begins to tremble violently, sweat sliding down his temples and the sides of his neck, his hand spasming in Brian's and his face screwing up.

"That's it," Brian breathes, thrusting faster. "Come around me, let go, sweetheart."

Kyle's ass clenches up so tightly when he shoots over Brian's fist that Brian comes not long after he does, whimpering and hammering up into him with frantic, deep thrusts.

They stay there pulsing and still for a long while, Kyle's body snug but not as tight as before around Brian's softening erection. He winces when Brian slides out of him, despite Brian going slow, and catches his breath as Brian discards the condom and gets them some tissues. He folds down onto Brian's chest after that, still shaking, and Brian holds him and strokes his back.

Brian knows how strange having another person inside of you can be, especially the first time. "Love you," he says into the quiet.

"Love you, too," Kyle replies.

"Are you okay? Was—was it okay?"

"I'm sore," Kyle admits, smiling against Brian's chest. He closes his eyes. "Is it cliché to feel different?"

"Not at all," Brian whispers, carding his fingers through Kyle's sweaty hair. "I do. Because you shared that with me, I feel different."

Kyle's smile widens. "I'm glad." He shifts onto the bed, leaving an arm and a leg over Brian's body. "It was different from what I expected. Weirder and drier and about a hundred times more intense."

"It's something you enjoy the more you do it. The more your body learns how to relax into it. You know, if it's something that you're going to enjoy at all. Not everyone does and that's totally okay. But if I—if I did something that you didn't like, please let me know."

"I'm pretty sure you did everything right," Kyle says, smiling. After a drowsy pause he asks, "Do you want to talk about what happened at the center?"

He doesn't, not particularly, but he does want Kyle to understand why he had to spend so much time at work. "Hulked-out vamp broke into the back rooms during the hour we were closed," he says. "Made one hell of a mess. One of the concealed security cameras survived his rampage," Brian answers. "He was a big boy. We didn't get much of a view beyond that, though. Just seconds of footage before something fell across the camera's lens."

"Was he looking for blood?"

"No, he went for the records. Computers, backup files. They still aren't sure what he got or even what he was looking for. Nothing was deleted or removed."

"That's odd."

"It really is. I could understand it if he were looking for blood; that's happened before. But what he actually did was so much worse. It'll be weeks before the center is up and running again, and in the meantime we have to set up temporary extensions at the uptown facility and fly in extra staff. I'll have to commute there for the time being. The shifts are going to be painful. We'll be working from digital backup data that may or may not be current, so we're going to have a lot of downtime ID-ing and serving. Vamps are going to get cranky, humans are going to get cranky—it's a recipe for disaster. But I guess we'll power through it. It was even messier when the centers first opened, so there is a precedent, at least."

Kyle smiles, tracing shapes on Brian's chest. "I can water your plants and take in your mail. I'll make sure there are groceries and things, too."

"You don't have to do all that," Brian replies, scratching his fingernails against Kyle's scalp. "But I'd appreciate it, if you could find the time." It's hard, letting someone else do things for him—he's always been very independent—but he has to start allowing Kyle to fill that space in his life. He wants that with Kyle, that level of trust and mutual care. "Erica made me agree to one day a week off, no matter what the shifts are like, so we'll have that and probably some daylight hours as well—it's just going to be crazy for a little while."

"I don't mind," Kyle says. "I've been taking extra clients. The money is good. Almost ready to start looking at used cars."

"Ooh," Brian hums. "Can I come with?"

Kyle laughs. "This is not my surprised face." He knows Brian has a lust for cars.

"I'll forgive the teasing as long as you say yes."

"Yes."

"Excellent."

"Will you eat breakfast now?" Kyle asks.

Brian grins. "Well, since you asked so nicely. And car shopping is hungry work."

The twin-sized bed in Kyle's room at the blood club is tiny. He considers this—but only peripherally—with his head buried between Brian's legs. He's kneeling on the floor beside the bed with Brian sitting across it horizontally, his ass hanging off the edge. Kyle switches from Brian's left to his right testicle with a wet slurp and a feral glance. He's been giving the ever-firming sacs very specific attention for almost a half an hour now.

Brian had gasped something that might have been a question about five minutes after Kyle pushed him down onto the mattress, and all Kyle had been able to offer by way of response was a growl that sounded like, "Love the way you taste." Which is the truth. There's something almost animal about the way he processes Brian's scent and flavor, and they make his mind buzz with lust and his mouth water.

His fangs aren't down but they want to be; his gums ache. He's so turned on it hurts—both to stop the fangs from dropping and to refrain from humping the heel of the palm he has pressed against his cock to keep from coming in his pants.

Brian's feet cling to the edge of the bed, his naked legs spread as wide as they can go, his cock and balls hanging flushed and heavy between them. Kyle supposes he should do something else, stroke Brian's cock or maybe go lower and lick him where he's twitching. But Kyle is drawn back to his spit-soaked balls again, finding them even tighter against his tongue now when he licks them from bottom to top and top to bottom.

Brian jerks, letting out a high-pitched noise that may or may not have been a word.

"Yeah?" Kyle teases, sucking his left ball between his lips and tonguing it.

"Oh my god, you are—so good at that."

He slides two fingertips across Brian's hole the next time he switches balls, and grins around his mouthful when Brian almost loses his footing on the metal edge of the bed frame.

"Kyle," Brian breathes, hips rocking desperately.

"Brian." He presses harder, drawing a circle around his wrinkled, swollen rim.

"*Please*," Brian answers, gripping the bedspread harder. "Please, there."

"Mm," Kyle hums. He's buzzing with power, knowing he could do anything right now and Brian would let him, would love it. Instincts that seem to prove accurate at every turn scream inside of him, telling him to lower his mouth to where Brian is opening up for him. He licks a broad stripe over the dark indent, and then another, growling in pleasure at the taste.

"Yes, please," Brian whimpers. He reaches down to wrap a hand around himself, but Kyle reaches up so quickly that his fingers blur. He grabs Brian's wrist a little too hard.

"Don't," he says. "Don't." He doesn't want Brian to get there, not yet.

"O-okay." Brian's eyes go hazy at the request, but he acquiesces.

Kyle works his tongue inside of Brian bit by bit until he's licking deep, his chin rubbing hard against Brian's spit-wet crack. He can't move much inside, it's so narrow and tight, but he can move his tongue in and out, in and out, taking time to suck and trace the puffy rim of Brian's hole with his lips before diving back inside. He doesn't keep track of the time. He doesn't do anything but chase that jerking, gasping reaction that he keeps earning, greedily wanting more and more of it.

He goes from feeling cheeky about how long he's drawing this out to just plain naughty, and before long they pass that sane foreplay mark and he keeps going until his mouth and the skin around it are numb. His jaw has started to twinge, which is amazing to feel—his body is built for unknown amounts of stamina, and to be pushing that limit must mean that Brian is well beyond normal sensitivity. He lifts his head to look at Brian, but keeps his cheeks spread with his thumbs. Brian's eyes are shut, his body drips sweat and his skin is flushed more or less everywhere. He looks unconscious.

Gently, Kyle edges the pad of his thumb along Brian's overheated, slick skin and finds his hole slack and soft. He pushes, firm and steady, and lets his thumb sink all the way inside.

Brian's eyes snap open. His throat works around a swallow. "*Please.* More."

Kyle applies a squirt of lubricant to his fingers, then pushes his pointer and middle finger back inside. He works the two digits in a quick series of short thrusts, unable to hear anything but the pounding of his heart and the wet noises that result. He stares, enthralled, at this gorgeous, close-up view of Brian's hole stretched and shining around his fingers.

Brian's pelvis stiffens with purpose as he works himself down around Kyle's fingers. His belly heaves but it's compressed, an adorable pinched roll of fat forming at the very bottom when he folds himself just so.

And then, without preamble, he gasps into the silence, "Fuck me. Need you to *fuck me*."

This is about all that Kyle can take; he's never heard Brian use language like that in bed before and the unfiltered thrill of it wrecks whatever patience he has left.

"Do you want it rough?" he asks, climbing up onto the bed and dragging Brian's pliant body into his lap. "I can be—I can do that." He's not sure why he's asking this, but it feels right.

Brian whimpers, straddling his lap and grabbing the back of his neck. "Yes. God, yes."

Kyle rushes into a condom, urgency clawing at the base of his spine; he wants to be inside Brian so badly that even rolling the latex on doesn't feel awkward.

Brian's face is so—soft, point to point against his, almost passive; he's given himself over completely to Kyle, and Kyle can't *breathe*, the power transfer feels so literal. Brian wraps his legs around him and Kyle tips them until Brian is under him, pinning Brian's arms above his head, and Brian whines, spreading out on the bed like an offering.

"Yeah," he says. Their eyes are locked, and his forearms flex against Kyle's fingers. "Hold me down. Hold me down and fuck me."

Kyle takes the right side of Brian's ass in hand, tips his pelvis higher and deeper into his lap and then guides his cock inside. There's no resistance as he pushes in, and this draws a guttural groan from him. He doesn't need to wait; Brian's body is beyond ready.

He doesn't look away when he begins to move. It's deep rolls at first, more grinding than thrusting, and then he simply gives over to his baser urges and lets his back and thighs go as he fucks Brian into the bed, making it shake so loudly that he's sure everyone in the building will figure out what they're doing. Strangely, that only makes him harder, only makes him fuck Brian faster, deeper, the noise of his balls slapping against Brian's skin driving him on.

"So tight," he growls, burying his face in Brian's underarm and licking the sweat there.

"Come on, come on, fuck me," Brian moans. Kyle holds his wrists tighter, leans closer, and presses him into the bed. He can feel Brian's cock, hard as a rock, trapped between them.

There are tears of exertion on Brian's cheeks. He can hardly breathe at the sight—Brian is so gorgeous like this, open and desperate and taking it. It's almost too much, so he closes his eyes and buries his face in Brian's shoulder.

The bed shakes. They breathe heavily together. Kyle listens to the slick noise of his cock spearing in and out of Brian's ass.

He feels a strange stab of urgency, and then—

"Bite me," Brian whimpers, tilting his jaw up. "Drink. Please. *Please.*" His fingers dig into Kyle's hair, tugging it hard enough that it would hurt if he were human. The almost-sting brings all the hair on Kyle's body to attention and he inhales sharply, his back bending.

He should think. He should slow down. But his fangs have dropped, and all he can feel is frantic desire riding atop an unconscious stream of *do it do it do it do it*. He isn't sure which of them is the source. He isn't sure if it matters.

He doesn't stop thrusting; he presses his face into the side of Brian's neck and bites, no questions, no worry, just does it—and only realizes when he hears Brian cry out that because he hasn't licked or kissed the skin, Brian will feel the full force and pain of the puncture. For a brief moment, he panics—should he stop? Should he keep going?

He's shocked to feel Brian wrench his right hand free and shove it between their sweaty bellies. He both feels and hears *don't stop don't stop keep drinking oh my god keep fucking me* as Brian jerks himself off frantically, pain and pleasure wracking his body. It only takes a minute or two for him to begin to thrash and sob, and then he comes suddenly, shooting all over them both, lush spurts of come that pool at his breastbone, drip down the sides of his torso and fleck his skin with pale splatter.

Oh my god, is all Kyle can think as he tries to keep his mouth tight around the wound. The effort comes just a second too late, and blood drips all over Brian's neck and shoulder and the bed but Brian doesn't seem to care; he clings tighter, stiff as a board but gasping into Kyle's hair. His body is content but still riding a painful high, a bliss that is beyond normal endurance levels and leaves his mind a mess of warm, soft edges that almost glow. Kyle can feel them, though he isn't sure how. For a moment he's frightened, and then he realizes that he's been halfway inside Brian's head for quite some time now.

He pulls back from the mental connection, or tries to. Where did that come from? He'd had no idea that he could do that. Is it mutual, or one way?

"Take more," Brian says, trying to recapture his attention. "I'm fine."

Fuck.

So he drinks. And drinks.

Brian only loosens his death grip when he lifts his mouth free to breathe. The room spins. Kyle's taken a lot of blood. Brian licks at the corner of his mouth and presses inside, dragging the tip of his tongue over and between Kyle's fangs. There's blood everywhere between their mouths, smearing sticky and dark and clotted.

Kyle hisses, rocking his hips. He's still hard, and as deep as Brian can take him. "Okay?"

"Yeah." Brian sweats more profusely than before, droplets rolling down his forehead and temples and neck. He doesn't seem to be suffering extreme discomfort, though. "That was incredible."

"You're weak," Kyle says, kissing down his throat. Brian's body is limp, and he just feels—fuzzy around the edges, to Kyle's senses. This doesn't stop Kyle from lifting his trembling thighs and moving inside of him again, though. "God, you're still so tight."

Brian whimpers. "If you—if you want to keep fucking me—I—you can."

But his body is *wrecked*, and now he's weak from blood loss.

"You're so tapped out," Kyle says. The observation is both an awed, aroused commentary and a question.

"Wh-what, what do you want?" he asks, so eager to satisfy. "I'll—you can do anything you want." His brown eyes are huge, their pupils blown wide open.

Kyle sits up on his knees, easing himself from the clench of Brian's body carefully, watching Brian's face tense as he's left empty. He knows what he wants: to kneel over Brian's chest, to snap the condom off and smooth a fist up the shaft of his throbbing cock. He breathes out, staring down at Brian's bloodstained face.

"I want you to swallow my come," he breathes, cupping Brian's jaw. "Every drop."

"Y-yes," Brian says, trembling.

It's the most shockingly erotic moment they've ever shared: Kyle jerking himself off with rapid strokes and Brian's throaty inhales and exhales as he waits, his mouth swollen and open.

"Come," Brian whimpers.

"Brian—"

"Come in my mouth," Brian begs, his lips trembling, his tongue licking the underside of the head hungrily.

Kyle lunges, pushing the head of his cock into Brian's mouth seconds before he spurts, and jolts of pearly come coat the roof of Brian's mouth. It just keeps happening, throb after throb after throb, Brian's fingernails digging into Kyle's thighs as he swallows. Kyle drags the head over Brian's tongue, forcing weak, secondary spurts to ooze across it. Brian's mouth goes soft and easy around Kyle, and then he drags his cock deeper, sucking the softening flesh deep into his mouth and drawing out whatever it has left to offer. Only when the sensation becomes a twinge does Kyle pop himself free.

"Could you stay there for a minute?" Brian asks, licking his mouth clean.

Kyle sits gingerly on his chest. "Sure."

His eyelids flutter shut again. "I—I've never—you are incredible. It's like you're in my head, like you know exactly what I want."

Kyle wonders if part of this is literally true. There have been moments between them, especially since they began to regularly work blood drinking into sex, when he has felt as if he could almost read Brian's mind. Or at least read his general mood, his ups and downs, well enough to understand his needs. Kyle has no idea of the extent to which vampires can do this, and Brian hasn't seemed to grasp the gravity of his observation, so he decides not to bring it up—at least not until he educates himself.

"I think I like it this way," he says, shifting the topic. "I like—" He blushes. "I like—"

"You like topping," Brian finishes for him, smiling.

"Is that okay?"

He worries about labeling it so definitively. He does enjoy having Brian inside of him, quite often; he likes feeling full and he likes having his ass touched. But being inside of Brian *thrills* him. It makes him feel like he belongs in his own skin, like his body is his instrument, like there isn't a thing that he couldn't accomplish in that moment and given that permission.

Brian grins. "In case it hasn't been obvious enough," he says, gaze going hot beneath his eyelashes, "I prefer bottoming."

Kyle whimpers at that. "But we can always switch. I don't want you to think—"

"I know, sweetheart. And we already have. It's a mood thing, you know? It's okay to want either or, and it's okay to agree on a preference."

"I guess so," Kyle says, his face still warm. It's silly that he can say and do all of these things to Brian, and then blush like a child when they talk about it afterward.

"Christ, are you two *done*?" comes Elisa's irritated voice from the other side of the door. "You've got a customer in twenty, *gato*."

Brian laughs, looking appropriately embarrassed. The wound on his neck isn't bleeding freely anymore, but it's messy and there's blood splatter all over his neck and side. "I'll clean up."

"Good idea," Kyle says, climbing off of him. "You smell too good right now. I might trail you home like a stray puppy." He shouts at the door, "Give me a minute."

"*Dios mio*," she grumbles, her heels clacking all the way down the hall.

"That's not much of an incentive," Brian says, walking shamelessly naked and filthy across the room. His body is a map of bruises and scratches and his shoulder looks as if it has been mauled.

"I hurt you," Kyle says, feeling guilty.

Brian glances down. "It looks worse than it is." He cleans the blood off of his skin with wet wipes from a bulk-sized box Kyle keeps. "Besides, I like the way it feels; when we're apart, it reminds me of you."

With the blood cleaned off, the wound looks as small as always; the neat bite marks and red-purple bruises the shape of Kyle's mouth will fade soon enough.

Kyle crosses the room to kiss him, savoring the glide of their lips before pulling back to stare into his eyes. "Stay until you're recovered, okay? First aid and pills are where we left them last time. And call me when you get home?"

Brian smiles at him, sweetly satiated. "I promise."

*

Elisa takes him clothes shopping.

He's become almost amazingly adept at getting her to spill details about her and Clara's lives before the club without asking direct questions (that way lie eye rolls and rapid-fire Spanish curse words).

So much about their lives, both past and present, is a mystery to him and, just when he thinks he's got them figured out, he realizes that he's way off the mark. Sometimes he overhears them talking about blood club business in ways that make it seem much bigger and more complicated than it appears to be. He's seen business suits and fancy luggage in their rooms, but he's never known them to attend meetings or go on business trips. Clara has odds and ends in her room that don't make sense to Kyle—goggles and lab coats mixed in with the little sundresses she's so fond of. Some rooms at the club are locked down so tight even he can't get into them, and he has no idea how they've managed that. Janice has become a good friend, but every time he tries to start a conversation with her about their selectively evasive employers, she shuts down completely. He's equal parts intrigued and worried about what all this might mean.

This time he uses a fashion choice Elisa makes to ask about her high school days.

She laughs, turning in front of the dressing room mirror. "I used to be crazy about uniforms, actually," she says. "Clara and I were on the softball team all through high school."

"Must've been a hell of a team."

"Mansford Borough High Wildflowers," she sings. "We were badass bitches."

Kyle stares straight ahead, trying not to allow the surprise to show on his face. He knows that they are much older than he is, and that there's probably a substantial time gap between their high school careers (and he went to Township, not Borough), but to hear the name of his hometown is unsettling, and an odd coincidence. Or is it? Sometimes he thinks that something other than pure chance had to lead to his collapse on their doorstep. Then again, he makes a habit of not believing in things that border too closely on spirituality.

"You're quiet," she says, adjusting her breasts in the mirror. "Does this combination not meet with your approval?"

"That pattern mismatch is so last season," he sighs.

She glares. "Never heard the phrase 'the hand that feeds you,' huh?"

"Just telling it like it is. Here, let me swap out that top." As he helps her button up a better choice, he asks, "I assume you were the fearless leader of this band of cheerful folks?"

"Depending on how bloodthirsty Clara was that week, yeah, sometimes," she answers, tugging the collar into place. "It was different then. I was dating someone else and she was dating the captain of the debate team."

"Wow!" Kyle steps back and tilts his head. "Better." He fusses with the shoes they've selected, holding them up to compare. "So how did you two end up together?"

She stares at him through their reflections. "You talk to her about this yet?"

"Uh, no." He tries to look as casually disinterested as possible. "Just curious. You're like my fairy godmothers."

Though she tries very hard to not look flattered, it's obvious that she is. "Well. *Of course*." She preens, taking the pair of shoes he holds out to her and sliding them on. "Long story short? My girlfriend didn't react well after I was turned. It—I scared her, once I became—this. And around the same time, Clara turned, too, and had a huge falling out with her idiot girlfriend. She hated it. Had all these plans for them and couldn't accept that Clara had changed. Bad enough being dykes, asking her to hide the vamp thing, too? Nah. It just wasn't her thing. And of course our families were assholes about it, hers especially. So we ended up in each other's arms, so to speak. It was all very *telenovela*."

"That's better," he says, referring to her outfit with a smile. He steps back as she begins to change. "You really love each other, though. I mean—it's sweet."

Elisa sighs, her eyes shifting away from his. "It took us a long time to get there, to build what we've got now. It wasn't always easy. She's—she's probably the only reason we made it. I can be kind of a hot mess."

Kyle slides his fingers down into hers. "Hey. You made it. You're together. That's all that matters, right?"

Something in her eyes tells him otherwise, but she says nothing and just tightens her fingers around his. He chalks up a win.

Later that day, he has dinner with Clara and brings up the one thing he'd forgotten to ask Elisa about earlier: the ability he seems to have to read Brian's mind.

"Sure," she replies. "We don't talk about it as a rule, obviously. If they knew that some of us were capable of that, we'd be in a bind, wouldn't we?" She stops to sip the blood in her wine glass, pushing a strand of hair off of her forehead. "It's not as developed as you'd like it to be. It only happens consistently when we drink, or before or after we drink. Or when we get close to a donor over time. I guess it helps to gauge their—well, how much we can take, how close they are to unconsciousness, stuff like that." She licks her lips. "You and Brian...?"

He blushes, fiddling with the napkin he's been tearing to shreds. "A little bit. He just thinks that I'm amazing at knowing what he wants when we're—" He motions politely.

She laughs. "Hey, honey. Nothing wrong with that." She raises her glass to him. "Enjoy."

"I don't want to read his mind against his will, though," he says, frowning. "And I don't feel like I have any control over it right now."

"You can turn it down, for the most part. Just visualize a wall between your minds. That usually does the trick for me."

He's not sure if he'd have enough control over himself in those moments to accomplish this, but if it will keep him from invading Brian's privacy he'll do his best.

They drink in peaceful silence together. Elisa floats through once or twice, stopping to tweak a strand of his hair and kiss Clara. Janice joins them for a while to discuss a scheduling issue before launching into a round of small talk. It's friendly and easy, and Kyle feels the warmth of their makeshift family settle in his bones.

When he and Clara are alone again, and the stack of papers beside her computer is almost gone, he asks, "Has there been anything else about the break-in at the center?"

"It's reopening on Monday, but I'm sure you knew that already," she says. "When the authorities are unable to solve a crime, they're very quiet about it. Case in point. Investigation dead in the water. Chances are the vamp was a rogue—sometimes they go nuts, monster strength and mental instability, the whole nine. The police will be happy to call it that and move on."

"I'm surprised that the backlash hasn't been more intense," Kyle says. "They usually love to use this kind of thing as an excuse to talk about what a threat we are."

She shrugs. "He didn't go for the blood. If he had it might've been different. As it is he only did damage to machines and paper. They're more embarrassed about not making an arrest than they are interested in throwing a weak punch at us. Chicago is pretty vamp-liberal right now." She watches him for a long moment. "Anything you need to tell me? Or was this just idle chit-chat?"

What to say to her?

He has no way of knowing for sure if this has anything to do with him. Since the beginning, he's panicked at the possibility that someone who knew Jeffrey might come looking for revenge. Vampires don't care about the human justice system; a vampire would find him, kill him and chop him into pieces. The police wouldn't pursue the matter. Even if they had a passing interest in his remains, they wouldn't be able to identify them because vampires decay differently than humans—they become flesh sludge within hours of death. So unless this vampire were kind enough to leave Kyle's wallet in the middle of his goo pile...

But who could it be? Jeffrey had had as few friends as Kyle did growing up, and there's no way anyone in his family could know what had happened that night at the school.

And then again, maybe Kyle is being extraordinarily paranoid and the break-in at the center has nothing to do with him.

"I'm concerned about people looking for me," he admits.

She *hmmphs* thoughtfully.

7

One thing Brian and Michael have always been able to enjoy together aside from tennis is shooting pool at the bar down the block from Michael's apartment. Before Michael turned, they used to drink beer and eat wings there at least once a month—now it's mostly pool and darts and Brian drinking twice the beer and eating twice the wings to make up for his brother's inability to do so. It doesn't hurt that it's always easier for Brian to hang out with Michael when he's buzzed. Tonight, he's well on his way to getting drunk.

The center is open again, but Erica has insisted that he take a week off before plunging back in full-time, so he's promised himself to make some time for the family and school friends he's been neglecting since he started dating Kyle.

He's musing about Kyle when Michael drags him out of from his thoughts with the announcement, "I'm going to ask Jenn to marry me."

He sets his beer bottle down and turns to face his brother. "Oh, gosh—that's wonderful."

"Since I made partner it's all I've thought about," he says. "Still kind of terrified, I have to admit."

"Don't be," Brian replies, patting him on the back. "She's crazy about you. You're crazy about each other."

"Assuming that she doesn't run screaming into the night and says yes—be my best man?"

Brian's throat closes up. He's sure that, just a year or two ago, he would not have been Michael's first choice for best man. The fact that he is now means the world to him.

"God, of course. *Of course* I will," he says, reaching for Michael.

They hug, and Michael ruffles his hair as they pull apart. "Thank god that's over." He grins. "Man, I miss getting drunk. That's probably the number one thing that I miss—well—hat and red meat." He stares off into space longingly, his jaw going slack. "Cheeseburgers."

Brian laughs. "You know, they're doing a study—"

"No," Michael groans. "Please, no. Not right now. We're doing so well. Don't ruin it."

"All right," he replies, grinning from ear to ear. He's so happy about being asked to be his brother's best man that he's willing to let it slide. For now. "Shutting up." He raises his beer bottle and clinks its neck against Michael's. "To wedded bliss."

They're sitting on a picnic blanket surrounded by shopping bags. Brian lost count somewhere around the sixth or seventh, too absorbed in trying to balance them and Kyle's hand in his while being pulled from vendor stall to vendor stall at the same time.

This arts and crafts show has been on their radar for weeks and, happily enough, falls during Brian's vacation week. Even though they've both been looking forward to it, it has been a long day, and he's tired. He's eaten a heavy, fried dinner, and now they are settled in the middle of a grassy field waiting for the fireworks to cap off the evening. Kyle nestles in front of him and sits back against his chest. Their hands are tangled in his lap.

He buries his face in Kyle's hair and breathes in the scent of it. "Had fun today?"

"God, yes," Kyle sighs, eyes tracing an arc across the dusky sky. "You?"

"So much fun," he answers.

"Oh, look," Kyle squeaks, pointing.

Purple and white bursts above them, and all at once the sky explodes into a cacophony of noise and light as the fireworks begin in earnest. Brian untangles one hand from Kyle's and strokes his fingers through Kyle's hair as they stare upward. They can't talk over the noise, so he spends most of the show watching the reflection of the fireworks flare across the surface of Kyle's wide, excited eyes.

He thinks about Michael asking Jenn to marry him. He knows that it's too soon for that kind of thinking as far as he and Kyle are concerned, but he definitely feels an urge to make things between them more defined, more permanent. It's a new feeling for him. Until now, he's been content to simply enjoy their time together. Kyle hasn't done anything to make him clingy, so what is it really about? It could be that he's going back to school soon—and that Kyle may very well be attending college as well. Once that starts, their time together will be drastically reduced. Maybe he's nervous about the effect that change will have on them. Maybe, once Kyle starts making friends and building a social life at whatever college or university he chooses, he'll meet someone else or change his mind about their relationship. Brian doesn't see what they have—doesn't see Kyle—being that flimsy, or as changeable—but that doesn't stop him from worrying about the possibilities.

When they're settled in bed later that night, his mind drifts to all the things he still doesn't know about Kyle. He can't even begin to plan settling down with Kyle, not with so much still on the table. He knows this, but it's difficult to swallow.

He twists onto his back, breathing out as Kyle's readjusts the arm resting across his chest. "Can I ask you something?"

A beat of hesitation makes Brian's stomach clench, but Kyle eventually replies, "Sure."

"How were you turned?" It's a good place to start; he knows that the answer isn't going to be pretty—sixteen is far too young to have been turned under healthy circumstances—but at least knowing the answer will be one more step toward understanding him.

He tenses but doesn't pull away. "It's not a happy story. Are you sure you want to hear it now?"

"Yes," Brian says. He doesn't want to ruin the day they've had, but this is important.

"I was always different, always stood out," Kyle begins. "You know, one of those kids who never had to come out because everyone just knew from day one. When I was little, before my parents died, they encouraged me to be myself and, well, I was. At least that's what I got from the nasty things my aunt and uncle used to say about my parents 'encouraging my unnatural habits.' Anyway, I, uh—I was picked on all through elementary and middle school. By the time I got to high school I was sort of used to it. All the kids who'd grown up knowing me as that flamboyant little kid who liked to wear colorful outfits and put on plays became the social climbers who were determined to keep me in my place. I, um, I did make some friends in drama club, but—I was awful at friendships in general."

Kyle inhales. Pauses. "I still wanted them, though. Sometimes I tried to fit in, or to reach out for attention when I got lonely, and one weekend there was a party. That's how these stupid high school tragedies always start, right? Such a stereotypical setup." He laughs, but it's empty. "The party was being thrown by an older brother of one of the drama kids. Some college students were there and I just—I was feeling rebellious, like I could handle myself no matter what. I got drunk and I ended up alone with one of the college guys." He breathes in. "I just wanted to be touched. I wanted someone to look at me as if I were—desirable, appealing, interesting, whatever. I wanted to know what it felt like."

Brian's heart begins to pound in a terrible rhythm. This isn't the story he'd expected to hear.

"He, um. He was very persistent, even though he didn't want to kiss me or do anything I wanted to do. He tried to—he wanted to—it—it didn't go very far, he just tried to, um. To get me to give him a handjob. When I refused, when I—pushed him off of me, he—he grabbed me and bit me. I knew that he was a vampire when I went with him. I mean I was just so stupid. I thought it would be sexy; I had all these dumb ideas about vampires and he seemed so nice at first. Anyway, he—he took too much blood. I don't know if it was because he was angry or horny or just clueless. He didn't know how to help me after, and the wound was too deep for the coagulant to stop the bleeding. Sheer dumb luck he didn't prick an artery.

"Anyway, he—panicked when I started to black out. When I woke up, the bed was covered in blood and I wasn't human anymore. He turned me to stop me from bleeding out, I guess. No one knew who he was. Just some random student from the college one county over. I never saw him again and no one—they all thought I deserved it for going upstairs with him. They told me that it was my fault. They made me sit through a vamp ed class, gave me some literature, assigned me time with the guidance counselor and that was that."

Kyle wipes furiously at his eyes. "The bullying changed—people knew I could hurt them, so they backed off physically. But the verbal stuff never stopped. They were experts at knowing just how much they could get away with. Eventually I learned how to hide myself better. I stopped trying to fit in, to make friends. I quit drama club."

When he stops speaking, Brian says, softly, "I had no idea."

Kyle looks up at him for the first time since he started telling the tale, and his eyes are swimming with tears. The eye contact seems to undo him; the tears spill over and keep spilling. His shoulders convulse.

Brian holds him until he's just sniffling. Brian doesn't want to say, "I'm sorry." He doesn't want to express the protective anger that has risen alongside that sorrow, either. He knows that expressing these feelings will not help Kyle or change anything.

"What happened to you is unforgivable," he whispers, his voice thick with emotion, "and not one bit of it is your fault." He pulls back, stroking Kyle's face. "You deserved so much more. But you're here. You're here, not only surviving but *thriving*, and I love you so much."

"I love you, too," Kyle answers, overwhelmed and on the verge of more tears. "You're right, I just—can we—not talk about it anymore tonight, please?"

"Not another word, I promise," Brian replies.

The next morning, the air between them feels so much more clear. Kyle was willing to open up; maybe he was waiting to be asked. That, Brian can deal with.

He goes out for fresh bread and orange juice and makes a detour to the local hardware store to get copies of his apartment keys made. Back at the apartment, he puts together a breakfast tray (bread, butter and jam and juice for himself, blood for Kyle). He uses a piece of butcher's string to tie the pair of keys to the hole at the top of the blood packet, carefully hiding them beneath it on the tray.

He thinks about the gesture he's about to make while a bed-headed, shirtless Kyle curls into his side and feeds him bites of bread. He sucks jam playfully from Kyle's fingertips while trying to judge his frame of mind. His eyes are red-rimmed from last night's crying but he seems happy now, and certainly happier than he was yesterday morning. Maybe talking about his turning was therapeutic for him? Maybe it was the thing he'd been so hesitant to discuss before? Brian isn't sure, but—the keys are already on the tray, and he doesn't intend to change his mind. It seems like the right time. He feels ready to make the offer.

Kyle reaches for the blood when Brian is finished eating. His eyebrows draw together in confusion when he feels the extra weight of the keys. They jingle loudly as he lifts them.

"I want you to be able to come and go, not just borrow my spare keys," Brian says nervously as Kyle turns the freshly cut metal between his fingers, his eyes widening. "I wouldn't mind coming home to you, sometimes. If that's something that you want, too, I mean; I want you to consider this place your home. You don't have to accept them, of course. I just thought—"

"I can keep these?" Kyle asks, voice breaking. "I can use them?"

Brian says, kissing him, "You're an important part of my life. I want you around as often as I can have you. Now that you have a car, it only makes sense that you can let yourself in when you get here, right?"

Kyle squeals and tackles him, catching the half-empty glass of orange juice and sticky, jam-covered plate that fly off of the tray with one hand, in midair, while the other frantically digs through Brian's hair to pull him into a fierce kiss.

"Thank you," he says, his eyes wet, his fingers shaking. "Thank you."

✷

The height of summer passes in a blur of activity; they take in everything the city has to offer, shows and concerts, movies and dancing, shopping and dining. Sometimes Kyle wonders how Brian manages to work, study and date him without dropping from exhaustion, but he never seems overwhelmed, so Kyle is happy to go with the flow.

He saves enough money for a semester's worth of modest college tuition and, with Elisa's help, manages to push through the paperwork to apply late for several performing arts programs in the area.

Jenn accepts Michael's marriage proposal and Kyle drives so that Brian, his brother and their friends can celebrate with a good old-fashioned pub crawl. Brian is a clingy, affectionate drunk, and though Kyle can't say that he's overly fond of handling Michael—who is very loud when out with a group of people, even though he can't get drunk—he's happy to be a part of the gathering. It seems like a real family, different from, but complementary to, the one he's become a part of at the blood club.

Toward the end of the evening, when Brian has begun to sober up, he tucks himself against Kyle's body as they stand under a street lamp and asks, "Be my date to the wedding?"

"Brian Preston, who else would you have taken?" Kyle asks, mock-scandalized as he jabs his boyfriend in the ribs.

"Formality." Brian's breath could knock out a horse. "God, I can't wait to see you in a suit. Will you let me buy you one? Please?" He grins, sliding his hands into the back pockets of Kyle's black jeans. "I promise to peel you out of it real slow. Piece." Kiss. "By piece." Kiss. "By piece."

There's no refusing *that*.

Another evening, Brian invites Kyle to meet some of his medical student friends, a mixed bag of amiable men and women who suggest they go to a gay-friendly club. They all dance and drink until the strobe lights are a blur and everyone smells, to Kyle, like sweat and blood. He experiences being checked out and hit on, really and truly, for the first time; it's a strange feeling, and he is simultaneously flattered and too overwhelmed to enjoy it.

"Can I try something?" Brian shouts over the music, loose from the cocktails his friends have been buying him. "Drop your teeth?"

"Here?" Kyle asks. "Why?"

"Humor me."

He does as requested and watches Brian drag the inside of his forearm over one sharp canine just hard enough to break the skin.

Kyle's nostrils flare and his pupils dilate at the smell. "Brian?"

Brian's face is sweaty. "Taste? I just want to see—"

Kyle doesn't need to be asked twice. He bends his head over Brian's arm and licks away the pinstripe of blood that's welled up. The cut is too shallow to offer more than a smear across his tongue, but the blood tastes good and makes his pulse stutter.

"Do you—is it any different than usual?" Brian asks, kissing his earlobe.

"A little," he replies, shivering. "But I'm not sure why." He drags his tongue over his gums. He feels a tingle, but he isn't sure whether it's the music or the dancing or the alcohol in Brian's blood.

"Sorry; science experiment." Brian's hands tighten on his hips and carry him into the next song.

Brian's friends have all either paired off or dispersed throughout the club, so Kyle doesn't see a reason not to do the same.

He still isn't sure if the music or atmosphere are suited to his taste, but there is nothing about rubbing up against Brian to a beat that he finds objectionable. Whatever doubts he has about the evening disappear when Brian's fingers tuck inside the waistband of his pants and they begin to move together. It feels good, though he's not very experienced at this kind of dancing, to give his body over to the rhythm that Brian helps to set, to tip his face up at the blinding, searching lights overhead and allow Brian's mouth to explore his neck. He forgets that they're two among hundreds. He stops noticing the stares tossed their way, and how other men try unsuccessfully to cut between them or bracket them.

It's a shock to his system when Brian shouts over the music, into his ear, "You have no idea how badly they want to put their hands on you, do you?"

His first reaction is, *I'm just some kid.*

But he has blossomed into a man under the warm glow of a respectful, mutual love, and that man is more aware of the effect he can have on others, just as he is aware that the outfit he's wearing—fashionable, but fitted to his body and arranged to show off all his assets—and the way he's writhing against Brian's body will draw attention.

The truth is, he was never "just some kid." The difference is that now, he's *sure* of that.

"Jealous?" he asks, grinning, though he already knows the answer.

"No," Brian answers, without a moment's hesitation, and it makes Kyle shiver. He loves that Brian isn't jealous. He loves that Brian is sure of him, of them.

Kyle kisses him, and the kiss goes from close-lipped to his tongue curling around Brian's in the space of three heartbeats. Brian's hands wrap around his back and pull him close.

"I'm yours," he breathes, wrapping his arms around Brian's neck.

He doesn't intend to let this dissolve into a trashy dance floor make-out session, but his moral high ground disappears, along with his hesitance to let go in public, when Brian's hands start to wander his back and shoulders; when a few kisses become a dozen; when their hips line up just right and Brian breathes out shakily against his lips, and he takes Brian's bottom lip between his teeth in reply.

Before he even realizes what he's doing, he's grinding their erections together through their pants, his fingers groping Brian's ass to get them closer together. The music, the crowd, Brian's friends—everything and everyone disappears but the two of them.

He can feel the bass line pounding in his bones, vibrating him right out of reality. The zing of Brian's blood is still alive in his mouth. He can taste it if he runs his tongue along the back of his teeth, and he knows that Brian knows it; there's a glint in his boyfriend's eyes—*You want more, I know you do, and I want to give it to you, I want to give it, give it, give it*—that pushes his instincts into overdrive.

He tongues hungrily over Brian's neck, all the way down to the spot where his skin is permanently flushed darker from the constant reapplication of Kyle's bite. He thinks that he hears Brian gasp his name but can't be sure, not with all this noise, so he closes his lips around the spot and *sucks*. Brian's body spasms under his hands.

Kyle's eyelids flutter shut. "Want you," comes tumbling out of his mouth when he lets it run, all breath and little forethought. "Want you so bad, want to *feel* you—take me home?"

Brian groans, holding him tighter. "Don't want to let you go."

"We can leave. We can—shit, your friends—" They're nice people. He doesn't want them to think he's some sex-crazed maniac.

"Give me five minutes," Brian says, and disappears.

Kyle isn't sure what excuses Brian makes for them, but ten minutes later they're jogging hand in hand back to Kyle's car, perfectly alone and giggling like kids as he wrestles with his keys. Brian takes over when he can't stop laughing, so Kyle latches onto him instead, kissing the back of his neck and putting his hands all over his chest and stomach. He nudges Brian into the driver's seat, grinning at the surprised noise Brian makes when Kyle straddles his lap, pushes the seat all the way back and closes the door behind them.

"Oh my god," Brian says, still laughing when Kyle spreads him out.

The screens on Kyle's windows—designed to block UV rays but still allow him to drive, more a defensive novelty than anything else (people tend to stay far away from vampires' cars)—serve the accidental, dual purpose of blocking a nighttime view of the inside of the car almost entirely. Kyle pulls them down one by one until the car is shrouded in darkness.

"Are you sure?" Brian gasps, as Kyle kisses him hungrily and fingers his jeans open.

"Need you," Kyle whines, shoving the material down around Brian's thighs.

"God, honey. Okay. Okay, let me—"

All they have is a tube of hand lotion and a crinkled condom that they rescue from the depths of Brian's wallet, but that will do.

Kyle pants, head thrown back, as Brian peels his pants and underwear off of his sweaty hips, then wraps one hand around his cock as it bobs free and uses the second to reach around behind him and spread him open.

"Right now?" Brian asks. "Right here?"

"Yes," Kyle says, hips churning. "Need it." He's so hungry for it that when Brian's fingers finally find him, he's already opening up. He whispers, thrusting down against them, "Come on."

Brian twists one finger inside, then a second when Kyle continues to whine. The slick squelch and tangy scent of the lotion drive Kyle's senses wild. He growls, rocking on Brian's fingers. It's never felt quite like this before, immediate and invasive but still not enough.

"Fuck me," he moans.

He's no longer embarrassed by the word—how could he be, with a condom between his fingers and Brian's cock in his hand?

It's quick after that, a frantic shuffle of sweat and skin as he sits up on Brian's pelvis and then sits down, seating himself carefully on Brian's cock. Even then it's almost not enough; he hates the lotion and the condom and wishes he could feel the drag of skin instead.

"Oh, god, baby, slow down," Brian chants, holding onto Kyle's hips for dear life as the car squeaks and rocks around them.

Kyle rises and falls, shoving his hands up and under Brian's shirt to get at his warm skin. "I don't want to use condoms anymore," he says, and Brian's eyes snap up to his. "I want to feel you." He bites his lip; Brian fucks up into him, hard and fast. His voice shakes. "I want you to come inside of me, want you to make me *wet*, want to feel it—feel it—f—oh, *fuck*."

"Kyle," Brian sobs.

"No one else's, I'm no one—else's—and you're mine and—I don't—want to use them anymore, okay?"

Brian groans, grabs Kyle around the waist, flips them over and pushes back inside, deep and rough, shoving Kyle's thighs up and apart.

"Spread yourself open for me—god, that's it."

Kyle whimpers and hooks his legs over Brian's shoulders. The weight of Brian's body behind his thrusts changes everything; the angle and pressure are suddenly perfect. Kyle lets himself open up and take it, lets himself savor the slap of their bodies coming together again and again as his fingernails scrape over Brian's back.

Brian comes inside him with a choked-off groan, hammering into him so fast, so erratically that the car doesn't seem to know in which direction to sway.

Kyle has one hand around his cock and tugs fast, ass tight around Brian. "I'm going to come, just stay, just—"

When he comes it's as messy and sudden as Brian's orgasm had been, splattering his hand and both their shirts, and Brian fucks him through it.

"Stay," Kyle breathes, heart pounding. "Stay in me."

"Did you mean that?" Brian asks, chasing his breath. "About the condoms?"

"Yeah." He pants. "You're the only one I want."

Brian's eyes go warm with pleasure. "I—same." Kyle kisses him. "So we'll get tested together—and then we'll stop."

He's still half-hard. The post-orgasmic throb feels good, and Kyle lets himself enjoy it, lets his body tighten and loosen around the intrusion still inside of him and watches Brian's face flicker with the sensation.

"You feel so good," he says, scattering kisses all over Brian's face and jaw. "I—it's never really felt like that before."

"Mm, I'm glad," Brian hums, pushing deeper. "Wish I could keep doing this for you." He's shrinking and the condom is going to slip off, so he has to pull out.

Kyle feels odd when he's gone, but cleans up between them while Brian continues to kiss his neck and shoulder. "Maybe later? Again?" he asks, a hopeful lilt in his tone.

Brian's eyes go dark. "When we get home, maybe?"

"Home it is," Kyle breathes.

After they get home, it's a blur again—Brian has him over the dining room table, the arm of the couch and the sink in the bathroom (they linger there for towels and a brief washing-up) before they even make it to the bed. There, Kyle employs all the restraint that he possesses so as not to rip Brian's clothing into pieces as they undress. (His club ensemble is actually rather darling; it would be a shame to destroy it, no matter how good the reason.)

Brian flips him onto his belly as soon as they hit the sheets naked, and before Kyle can even gasp out what he wants, Brian is spreading him open and licking down and over his swollen hole. The softness of his tongue is soothing after all the friction, but the moment he starts licking inside, Kyle needs more. The tickle of his tongue is not enough.

"Again," he pants, sticking his ass in the air. Brian kneels up behind him and fills him with one quick thrust. Kyle groans, wrapping his hands around the top of the headboard and holding onto it as Brian fucks him. It feels amazing, but the angle isn't doing what Kyle wants it to do, so after a minute or two he asks, "Let me on top?"

Brian huffs, winded, "Okay."

A moment of slippery rearrangement, and Kyle sits down on Brian's cock with a high-pitched snarl and slams forward, his eyes rolling back in his head. "Oh *god* yes, push up, just like that," he groans. He puts one hand back on the headboard and rides Brian into the mattress. "Don't move don't move—just—let me—second—"

"Yeah," Brian breathes. "Do what feels good."

It feels better than good—it feels *perfect* in a way that it never has before; the stretch, the flutter in his belly and the thrust of a cock in his ass all making the rest of his body vibrate with completion. Every part of him wants this.

He rocks forward and back dozens of times, finding a rhythm that does something to his prostate he's never managed to get Brian's cock to do before. His own cock juts up, pulsing and swollen and wet at the tip, and oh, god, he's going to come so *hard*—

He doesn't even have the words to warn Brian, it's that fast; one moment he's grinding down against Brian's cock and the next he's shooting thick, creamy strands of come all over Brian's chest without a single touch to help him along.

"Oh my *god*," he cries, quivering so hard he almost slips sideways. Brian keeps fucking him, deep and slow, milking him of several more pulses until there's nothing left; and only then does Brian allow himself to come with a groan, filling the condom. "Shit," he whimpers, every muscle in his body ticking. "How did I do that?" Brian laughs, still trying to catch his breath. They are covered in bodily fluids. Kyle wrinkles his nose. "Have a hose handy?"

"Will a shower do?"

Kyle bites his lip and smiles blissfully into the darkness of the bedroom. "It'll have to."

They attempt another go in the shower, but cleanup takes priority when they realize that it's not physically possible for either of them.

Of course, they've perfected one intimacy that has nothing to do with that...

Brian nibbles Kyle's ear and presses him into the tiles, one hand buried in his wet hair. Kyle kisses at Brian's wrist and forearm, and before he can control it, his fangs drop.

Brian notices and kisses higher along the ridge of his ear. "Go ahead."

Kyle bites down on the soft flesh of Brian's inner arm, staying away from the earlier cut, and is immediately lost to a rush of sensation as the blood spills past his lips. Some escapes down his chin, but he clamps tighter to stop that from happening and moans into Brian's skin as steam rises around them, making the smell of blood even stronger.

Brian whimpers and presses his arm to Kyle's mouth. Kyle can feel his willingness, can feel how intense his desire is to give Kyle his blood; this is almost as overwhelming as the blood itself. He pulls away after a short while, letting the coagulant do its job away from the shower's spray while he rinses the excess blood from his mouth and face. Brian intercepts him before he finishes, kissing him until their lips are smeared with it; and he only cleans them off completely once he's had his fill of coppery kisses.

Kyle smiles at him. "Thank you."

"My pleasure," he replies.

8

Even though he has a car now, Kyle still likes to explore the city on foot. When he isn't with Brian, his routine is simple: he takes clients, spends time with Elisa or Clara or Janice, texts Brian to check in with him, and then picks a direction and just walks.

One of the advantages of being a vampire is that he doesn't have to worry about humans messing with him. Other vampires treat him with caution; there's no way of knowing at a glance how old or strong another vampire is, so they tend to give each other a wide berth.

He's stumbled upon so many interesting things this way: shops, people, businesses, even other blood clubs. Social interaction is still something he prefers to take in small, controlled doses, but from time to time it feels good to interact with new people, sometimes even other vampires, whether it earns him a nod or a smile or a "Cool tonight, isn't it?"

He spends a lot of this time thinking—mostly about Brian, of course. He also thinks about the secrets he carries in shame and constant terror of their potential revelation. He thinks about the two performing arts schools that have accepted his application (neither are his top choices but, considering that he'd had to patch together a false identity and applied late, these are small miracles for which is he grateful). He thinks about the end of the summer, and about his soon-to-be schedule and Brian's, combining to reveal a worrisome lack of time for one another.

He thinks about the two new keys on his key ring. He shifts his fingertips over them inside his pocket, one and then the other, taking care to not squeeze hard enough to bend them, which he could easily do. Such a simple thing, a pair of keys, but they mean the world to him now, and every time he worries about the future he touches them and is reminded of everything in his life that is good and happy and whole.

And whatever happens, he will never regret falling in love with Brian.

Erica's email has no subject line, but it does have an attachment and the body reads, "You might want to look at this. I was online looking for articles about the incident at the clinic and came across this. I debated sending it to you, but you have the right to know, Bri."

It's a link to a missing person bulletin from a popular Chicago newspaper's website. Brian reads it with his stomach in his bowels and his heart beating an ugly tattoo against the inside of his chest. Once the initial shock fades, he moves from his desk to the couch in his living room and sits there completely frozen, staring at nothing.

What—or whom—has Kyle left behind, and under what circumstances?

What hasn't Kyle told him?

He calls Erica when he's recovered enough to speak coherently.

"Can you find coverage for me tonight?" he asks. He knows it's an inconvenience, especially considering that he swapped shifts today as a favor for someone else. "I have to talk to him. In person. I'm not sure how long it'll take, and I want to give this the time that it deserves. It can't wait. It's waited long enough as it is."

He can hear the concern in her voice when she replies, "I'll figure something out. Just—tread lightly, okay?"

"I will. Love you. You know that, right?"

"Yeah, yeah, you big mush. Love you, too."

Kyle doesn't answer his first call or text, but that's not unusual. Sometimes he's busy with clients, and at other times he flat out forgets that he has a cell phone.

Brian drives to the blood club, where Janice tells him that Kyle went out hours ago and hadn't mentioned when he'd be back. Brian isn't about to wander the city on the off chance that Kyle decides to pass through a familiar haunt, but he does pace the few blocks around the club twice over, kicking at the sidewalk and letting his mind race.

Dread wells, black and sucking, at the center of his chest.

What if Kyle's past is something that he simply can't live with, or something that they can't endure as a couple? The doubt is so thick within him now, he can't breathe, To have come so far, to have fallen so deeply in love with this man, only to have this potential ripped away—

He just doesn't *know*, and it's driving him insane.

It's the last thing that he thinks before something—or someone—comes out of the shadows of the alley behind him and knocks him down, turning the world dark.

Kyle drops by the center without calling first, which isn't usually an issue. He gets in line for blood out of habit, but all he wants is to talk to Brian. When he reaches the front of the line, he notices an unfamiliar face on Brian's side of the counter, so he switches to Erica's line and waits for a chance to speak to her, instead.

"Wasn't Brian working tonight?" he asks after saying hello.

"Could you step off to the side?" she asks, looking stressed. When he does, she frowns at him. "He—he went looking for you. He called in earlier."

Kyle's chest seizes up with ice-cold fear. "Did he say why? We didn't have plans."

"Kyle," she sighs, glancing at the vampire next in line, who is looking impatient. "Find him. Talk to him. Please. It's none of my business, and I don't want to play go-between."

Fuck. *Fuck*.

He fumbles for his phone. There are two missed calls and a text message from Brian asking him where he is, and would he be able to come back to the club to talk? No voicemail.

"Thanks," he says, and scurries to get out of the way.

"Asshole," mutters the vampire in line behind him. He doesn't even stop to glare in response.

He blurs his way back to the blood club, heedless of the energy drain—he hasn't eaten today, so it takes a lot out of him—and the wave of ruffled pedestrians he leaves behind.

The evening shift has taken over, but Janice has left a note on his door that reads, "Your boy came looking for you a few hours ago. Answer your phone, dummy! xoxo J."

Shit.

What could Brian need to discuss with him so urgently that he would come looking for him without speaking to him first, and then speed off to continue the search the moment he couldn't find him? It isn't like Brian not to plan things ahead of time, and if he begged off work on a moment's notice it has to be something serious.

And he isn't answering his phone.

Now the panic begins in earnest, bubbling up inside Kyle like a poison from the deepest, darkest parts of himself. He can't shake the feeling that this is it—somehow, Brian has found out why he fled Mansford and wants to break things off with him as soon as possible. He wouldn't be able to blame him if he did.

And there's another layer: a sharp-edged worry unrelated to his crime being exposed—he can deal with that; he can even deal with the thought of Brian's reaction, because he *did* those things and the consequences are his to bear. He's been preparing himself for some time; even though the outcome might break him, he can only blame himself. But there's something else. Something that has to do with Brian and the circumstances of this evening, with the way their communication has broken down.

He paces the streets around the club, redialing Brian's number again and again and again. He's tempted to call Michael or Jenn, but he doesn't want to worry Brian's family unnecessarily.

But for Brian not to answer his calls after having looked for him so frantically...

Something is wrong. It all boils down to that knowledge, deep and instinctive in Kyle's gut. Something is very wrong.

*

It's the first time Brian's been bitten against his will, and he learns firsthand why people who have gone through it look as though they've been mauled—it's a far cry from the neat, precise slide of teeth he receives when Kyle takes him in the most loving way possible. It feels as if his throat has been ripped open, and there is nothing he can do. Before he can even attempt to struggle, he's badly wounded and sliding into unconsciousness, Kyle's name a silent scream reverberating in his head.

Kyle is halfway back to the center when he feels it—vertigo, thick with human fear, the smell of it like the smell of blood when Brian is excited, only tinged with something foul: a smoky residue, sharp and reeking and coating the usually eager notes with unbridled terror. Brian's not alone, and the source of his fear is the vampire who is with him.

Brian is in trouble. Brian is hurt. Their connection isn't complete enough to tell Kyle exactly where he is or even when he'd been attacked, but it does give him a sense of Brian's location, and that's a start. He latches onto the sensation and moves in its general direction. After several minor course adjustments, he believes he's heading in the right direction. By then he's on the phone to Elisa, not stopping or even slowing down.

"I need your help," he says, when she answers.

"Look, I told you, it happens to a lot of humans—"

"Elisa," he growls, dashing the space of two city blocks in one push. "Brian's been attacked by a vampire. I felt him go unconscious."

"Where are you?" she asks, instantly serious.

"The little bodega, the one that Andrew gets those enchiladas from."

"Where are you *headed*?"

He can hear her shuffling; she shouts something, and then he hears Clara's voice in the background. "East. From the blood center. Can you keep up?"

"Oh, please," she growls, and the line goes dead.

Calling the police would be pointless. They'd never get there in time, and even if they did, they'd be useless. He recalls the description of the vampire responsible for the break-in at the center, and his mind whirls yet again but fails to make a connection. And if Brian has been attacked by this vampire the situation is too dangerous to involve humans, anyway.

For a split second he thinks of Michael again, but no. It wouldn't be fair to scare him like that, and god only knows what he'd do to catch up with them—he lives on the other side of the city and isn't often available at this time of night. Kyle can't afford to waste the focus that a second phone call would require, much less the time he might lose trying to meet up with Elisa and Clara *and* Michael.

He's already made his choice. He hopes it's the right one.

It's a park Kyle has never been to. This makes him nervous, though the feeling has less to do with the unfamiliarity of the terrain than with the open air; the boundary-free nature of the setting concerns him. The vampire and Brian could be anywhere, possibly moving faster than he can; a building or the partial containment of the urban landscape might have provided some limits to the engagement.

He can smell Brian's blood now, and sense the trembling riffs of Brian's semiconscious thoughts. Closer is better; the location becomes clearer in his mind, and he's across the park in seconds. With every blur of speed he feels a little less on top of his game, which worries him—he had intended to feed on Brian tonight but the reserves he has here and now are all he will have to work with.

He finds Elisa and Clara quickly, relief palpable in the air between them as they come together under the cover of darkness. The two women look deadly and efficient in black clothing and running shoes, outfits so unlike their usual turnout that Kyle can only stare at them. They mean business, and he's so glad to have them by his side.

"Have you locked onto him yet?" Elisa asks, moving alongside him.

He hadn't stopped to greet them, though he needs a moment before he can blur again; at least in the meantime he can keep moving toward Brian's scent and make some progress.

"I think so," he answers, as Clara falls into step at his other side.

"Is he bleeding out?" she asks, nose to the air.

"He's bleeding, but he's not that far gone yet, no," he answers. He feels a rush of strength, so he quickly pushes a blur that takes him another half-mile through the trees. The women blur with him and fan out to his sides. Three sets of vampiric eyes are much better than one, and they have their immediate surroundings memorized in short order.

"I've been here before. There's a visitor's center with a path that leads down to a fishing spot," Clara says.

"That way?" Kyle asks, because that is absolutely the right direction.

She nods and he blurs again, fear making him desperate.

None of Brian's training prepared him for this. He's interacted with every kind of vampire imaginable, but never been in a situation where he was both defenseless and denied the opportunity to reason with one. Nothing he says seems to make sense to his captor; or perhaps the vampire is just not listening.

Brian is growing sleepier by the minute. He's lost a lot of blood. He's also feeling remarkably stupid—he's sure he could have done *something* to keep himself out of harm's way, though what that is exactly he doesn't know. He's also frightened.

When he'd first come to, he thought the vampire might just feed from him and leave him for dead. The anticoagulant had never fully kicked in, though, and then, instead of dropping him like an empty soda can, the vampire had started babbling about finding him, finally, and about getting him to the park.

Brian has no idea what he wants, but it isn't to kill him—at least, not yet—because the vampire prods him awake every time he nods off. He supposes he should be grateful. He isn't sure exactly how much blood he's lost, but it seems to be a lot. He can't feel the wound anymore, and that scares him more than anything. He'd managed to jam his hand against it for a while, but then his fingers had grown so slippery with blood that it wasn't possible to continue, not with his strength leaving him so quickly.

He stares blearily at the young man pacing in front of him. It's hard to focus enough to catalog details, but he's a stocky guy with short dark hair, covered in blood from his mouth to the neck of his t-shirt. Brian's blood. He's turning frantic circles and muttering to himself.

In an effort to stay conscious, Brian tries to recall details.

There had been a building, at first, rectangular and dark and smelling of charred firewood—but then, as time passed, the vampire seemed to grow dissatisfied with his choice and had dragged Brian down a path covered in wooden planks to the edge of a fishing pond, which is where they are now. It's man-made and smells briny, and he *knows* this place—but he can't make the pieces slot together. His thoughts refuse to remain ordered, and he's so cold.

And then something changes.

The vampire rushes up the hill and then back down, a two-way blur that takes only seconds and makes Brian's body twitch with fear. He's so fast, so strong—but there's something wrong with him, and whatever it is, it's terrifying.

"He's close," the vampire says, and if Brian weren't so out of it, he'd be sure that the vampire is crying.

"We rarely get to play the element-of-surprise card with each other. If I can smell him, he can smell us," Elisa explains, leading them down the slope of the hill.

"Suggestions?" he asks. He's prepared to fight; he has almost no experience doing so, but he will do anything for Brian, up to and including putting himself in mortal danger if there is even the faintest hope of saving Brian's life in the process.

"Depends on his goals," Clara whispers, leading Kyle forward through the trees. "If he wants Brian for food, he may drop him and give up at the first sign of competition. If he wants Brian for a reason—he may just snap his neck the moment he gets whatever he wants." Kyle winces, and Elisa sighs impatiently. "Sorry. It's the truth. We have to play this smart."

They come out of the trees. The visitor's center is right in front of them.

"We've got numbers on our side," Elisa says, climbing over a tangle of brush piled high behind the building. There's a window, but the room it opens onto is black as pitch. "Keep the structure between us, and draw him away from the water—Kyle, find Brian and get him the hell out of here. Elisa and I can take the vamp, scare him or chase him or mess him up if he decides to try anything."

"I don't want you guys getting hurt because of me," Kyle blurts, his panic setting in again; he's torn between doing what she says to ensure Brian's safety and his loyalty to her and Clara.

"Fucking hell," Elisa drawls, rolling her eyes. "Do we look like newbies to you? Go get your doctor."

It's no longer a matter of choice; Kyle can hear Brian's sluggish, frightened thoughts now, can smell the trail of his blood all over the path they're walking on, and inside of the building and beyond, and it's too much. He has to find Brian and take him away. He can't wait any longer.

"When we've got him at a distance, blur your skinny ass over to Brian, grab him and blur across the water if you can manage it. Give it everything you've got; we can't go all *Jesus Christ Superstar* on water as far as I know, so speed is your best friend right now," Elisa says.

He goes, numb but determined.

It all goes to hell the second they split up. The vampire does drift far enough away from Brian for Clara and Elisa to get his attention, but not for long enough.

Kyle finds Brian by the water and has him in his arms in seconds, but he is seriously injured. The left side of his neck is torn open from no less than three major bites and countless minor ones, and he's so weak now, so far gone, that his mind is starting to lose its distinctive shape and color within Kyle's own. Kyle feels the panic jab deeper: the need to be away, the need to save Brian—how can he do both at once?

He hesitates—what if blurring across the lake with Brian now pushes him beyond help?

His hesitation costs them the plan. Once he realizes he's facing multiple enemies, the vampire is back at Brian's side in seconds.

For a second, Kyle can't process what's in front of him. He stares blankly up into the face of Jeffrey Simmons and hesitates a second time—not because it's Jeffrey, and not because Jeffrey is very much alive and staring at him with a mixture of longing and rage so disturbing it makes Kyle want to puke, but because he can feel and hear every whirling thought in Jeffrey's head.

Jeffrey is his. His creation. And the inside of Jeffrey's head is the most revolting thing he has ever experienced. He stumbles back, shielding Brian with his body, but it's not enough. He's not strong enough. He has screwed up, and now they are all in danger.

"I knew you'd come for him," Jeffrey says, his eyes wild, his mouth wet with bloody saliva. He smells like rotting meat.

Elisa and Clara appear at the foot of the hill and stalk quietly up behind Jeffrey. One wrong move and this will devolve into a bloodbath, and they know it. They hang back in silence while Kyle tries to keep Brian hidden. He stares at Jeffrey in morbid fascination.

"I killed you," he says.

Jeffrey holds up his arms and puffs out his chest. "Do I look dead to you?" It's an odd moment of sarcastic clarity considering the confused cesspool that is his mind.

Behind him, Elisa stares at Kyle.

Kyle can hear Brian moan and try to sit up. Every nerve in his body jolts with the urge to grab him and run, but he can't. Until today he'd thought himself a murderer, and the revelation that he isn't one sings through him with just as much relief as confusion. If he leaves now, he'll never know what really happened the night he escaped. And, in any case, Jeffrey has to be dealt with. Until then, Brian will remain in danger.

"When I woke up, you were gone, and I thought it was some kind of test," Jeffrey says, staring at him in that strange, intimate way. "So I—I manned up and went looking for you. Couldn't find you, but always felt you just—on the edge of my mind." He jabs his temple with a shaking, bloody finger. "I get here, man, and what do I find? You got yourself this puny, worthless meatbag for a b-boyfriend—"

Kyle's head aches. "*You* did that, Jeffrey. You tied me up and you cut me open and you drank my blood."

Clara twitches closer, her eyes dancing with warning. Kyle knows that she's trying to tell him to back down—that the truth is not what Jeffrey wants to hear. She's right. So instead, he tries to find something, anything in Jeffrey's thoughts that feels rational—something he can grab onto and use to reach him before he snaps completely.

He can feel the urgency in Elisa and Clara, willing him to be careful of the bloodthirsty, possessive anger inside Jeffrey, willing him to *understand*, and below all of that strength and noise he can feel Brian's ever-weakening will to stay awake. This is going to end badly if he does or says the wrong thing and he can't let that happen, not with Brian slipping away.

"I had no idea that you survived," he says, finally. "If I had, I wouldn't have left you." That much is true. "I didn't want to get in trouble, Jeffrey. You understand don't you? I thought I'd killed you."

Jeffrey's face contorts with anguished affection. He takes a step towards Kyle. "You were always one step ahead of me. I got blood at that—clinic—and I smelled you all over him. I saw your marks on him, but I could never get to him when he was alone. I had to get your attention, Kyle, I had to make you understand—see how *weak* he is. How unworthy. People like that, they aren't right for us. That's why I—did what I did. So I could be strong like you. So that you would see how—perfect we could be together, once I wasn't that pathetic human anymore." He glances at Elisa and Clara. "Who—who are they?"

"Friends," Kyle says, quickly. "Don't worry about them."

He could make a break for it with Brian right now, but Jeffrey would only follow; he'd still risk Brian's life in the process. Or he could let Elisa and Clara take Brian to safety while he continues to play for time with Jeffrey. He doesn't want to; he has to.

"You didn't have to hurt anyone," he says, careful not to mention Brian's name or even look at him. "But it's okay. I really want to talk with you, in private. Okay? Can we do that?"

"Just you and me, right? Not—not them?" Jeffrey asks, pointing to Elisa and Clara.

Elisa's eyes go wide. Clara twitches and steps forward. Their body language screams *no*. But they don't understand. They can't feel the synapses misfiring in Jeffrey's mind. He's not going to let Brian go unless he knows he has Kyle's undivided attention. He doesn't even see Brian as a being on the same level of existence—it would be nothing to him to snap Brian in half. He wouldn't understand what the big deal was, or why Kyle would continue to care once Brian was gone. Separating Brian and Jeffrey peacefully now is the only way to ensure that Brian has a chance of surviving. They're running out of time.

"Yeah, just the two of us," he replies. He stares at Elisa, pleading without words. Clara glances at her, and she glances at Clara, and they look terrified but move forward all the same. Elisa hoists Brian in her arms. He moans and twists, his fists opening in an attempt at self-defense. It's like being driven full of knives for Kyle not to turn and look, not to reach for him as Elisa carries him away.

Clara lingers a step behind, looking at Kyle and then Jeffrey. Kyle wills her to not do anything that will jeopardize Brian's escape. She steps close and puts her hand on his arm, and he feels the dig of her fingernail. She breaks his skin, just enough to make him bleed, so subtly that, with all of the human blood scent around, Jeffrey would never notice.

He hears her in his head, as clearly as if she were speaking out loud. *We can't take Brian to a hospital—they'd ask too many questions—but we have something just as good on tap. Go back to the blood club. Do not let this kid out of your sight—**bring him with you**.*

Kyle tries as best as he can to project agreement without allowing Jeffrey to feel it.

And then they're alone.

The moment Brian is out of Jeffrey's range, cold relief snaps through Kyle. Brian is going to get help; and now that this is accomplished, his courage is leaving him. He wants to *stop*, but he can't. In fact, he's going to have to give the most convincing performance of his life tonight. This ordeal is far from over.

He turns to Jeffrey, squaring his shoulders. "Come with me?" he asks, holding out a hand.

Jeffrey's face splits in a wobbly, broken smile that makes the hair on the back of Kyle's neck stand up. He takes Kyle's hand.

✷

Flashing lights. The smell of blood. Disorientation.

Something snaps inside him when he realizes that he has no idea where he is, that he should hurt but doesn't, and that he feels as if he has been near Kyle but it could have been a hallucination. Not knowing where or how he is makes him go a little crazy. He feels as if he's drowning inside of his own head.

"Where's Kyle?" he keeps asking, or at least he thinks he is. His limbs try to flail to get attention, but his body isn't listening. "Please, take me to Kyle, where is Kyle?"

"Get him on the table," comes a familiar voice. Brian should know who it is, but he can't think. Why aren't they listening to him?

"Give me something, Szeto—"

"If you leave me to it he'll be fine, but I need to work; he's lost a lot of blood. *Move*."

"That's all I needed to know," Elisa says.

"I have to get back to the club," Clara says.

Erica. Elisa. Clara. Oh, thank god.

Brian goes limp with relief. He floats for a while, misses part of the conversation, and then has the strength to listen again.

"You didn't have time to explain—"

"No," Clara replies, sounding worried. "Even if I had, if Kyle knew, then Jeffrey would have gotten it from him; Kyle is his maker, and Jeffrey is *freakishly* perceptive in a completely unpredictable way—I had no idea what he'd get from Kyle or how well Kyle has learned to shield. Should have trained him. Shit. Too late now. I'm going to give Kyle time to get his guard down, and then—we'll put it to the test."

Elisa sighs. "I knew we should've tested it sooner."

"It was item number thirty-three on the list," Clara hisses. "How could we have known we'd need it tonight?"

“Should’ve probably had a higher priority,” Elisa muses. “Shit’s pretty badass.”

There’s a pause, and then Clara says, “Spilled milk.” She moves farther away. “I’ve got the cloaking device, so I’ll leave a trail for him, but I can only say so much. He can’t know what he’s leading Jeffrey into, and if Jeffrey finds out that I’m there—we’re screwed.”

A wave of pain washes over Brian, flaring like a strobe light behind his eyes. It drownss him, and he passes out.

He can’t think of anywhere he’d like to take Jeffrey less than the place that’s been his home and refuge all summer. But Clara was adamant, and he can’t think of anywhere else that he knows better; he supposes that home field advantage wins the day.

Jeffrey is by no means calm, but Kyle has held his blood-sticky hand all the way, and he seems quieter than he was when they first saw each other. Deep down inside, in a place he muffles with every fiber of his being, Kyle is *screaming*. But he has a job to do, and if he does it well, this nightmare might actually end soon.

“You’ve been here this whole time?” Jeffrey asks.

“Yes,” he says, leading Jeffrey inside. He isn’t sure how Clara has managed it, but the building is deserted.

“I could never get into any of the buildings on this block without getting caught,” Jeffrey says, gawking as Kyle leads him upstairs.

He isn’t sure what Clara wants him to do, but where else would be a more likely starting point than his own room?

“You got into the clinic,” he points out, trying to sound interested instead of accusatory.

“I was so mad that night,” Jeffrey admits. “I tried to look for your name in the computer but I couldn’t figure out how to find anything.”

“I’m not registered there,” Kyle says, forcing a smile. “Not under my real name, I mean.”

“I gave up. That’s when I got really mad.” His face is blank with an ice-cold anger that makes Kyle want to let go of his hand and put space between them; but of course he can’t do that.

"This is my room," he says, trying not to waver.

A quick scan for something, anything, different in the room reveals a slip of paper on his desk that wasn't there when he left. He palms the note before Jeffrey can notice, turning his back and opening the window shade to let in the light from the streetlamp so that he can read it.

I think our guest might enjoy the basement; your favorite chair is so comfy. Remember our little chat about walls.

He recognizes Clara's handwriting, so she must be somewhere in or near the building, but he can't sense her at all. And what does she mean? He gets the bit about shielding; he's been trying to keep his thoughts boxed up and separate from Jeffrey's, but why the basement and what does she mean, mentioning the chair he likes to sit in when he's downstairs?

He slides the paper under a book on his desk and turns to Jeffrey, who is sitting on his bed. His skin crawls—he's made love to Brian in that bed, and now the vampire who had almost killed him and is still covered in his blood is just *sitting* there, as if he has the right.

Kyle takes a deep breath. "Can I get you some blood?"

"Sure. Yeah."

With every moment that passes, he feels more agitated. The pulse of sickening desire for him that rises from Jeffrey like smoke makes him want to twitch out of his own skin to escape it. And between these notes are sickening flashes of the humans Jeffrey killed on his way to find him—several of them young men who reminded him of Kyle—and the things he thought as he killed them—

Kyle breathes in through his nose. He can't lose it now, not when he's so close to executing whatever plan Clara has devised. This building is her fortress, and he trusts her completely.

Jeffrey sucks down several blood packets of varying types—he doesn't seem to know or care about matches, and he doesn't show any negative side effects afterward. Now he'll be more likely to agree to whatever Kyle suggests.

Kyle has to get him downstairs, but how?

"It's really cramped up here," he says, sitting on the bed beside Jeffrey. He puts on the sweetest, most open expression he can muster, allowing his honest desire to take Jeffrey downstairs shine through. "There's a finished basement—like a common room? With a pool table and a television. We could talk there. We're the only ones here tonight."

He lowers his eyes. The implication makes him want to throw up, but he plays it out of necessity, tracing Jeffrey's knuckles with his fingertips.

"I'm so glad you understand," Jeffrey says, and there's that smile again, and then his fingers trail clumsily along Kyle's arm. "So glad."

Kyle leads Jeffrey through the building, on the alert for any sign of Clara—it's so odd that he can't feel her when he knows that she must be around. Downstairs, he squares his shoulders and leads Jeffrey in the direction of the armchair.

"This is my favorite place to sit," he says. This much is true, and clearly puts Jeffrey at ease. "Why don't you relax? I'll get us some more blood."

Kyle holds his breath as Jeffrey sits down. He doesn't know exactly which instinct tells him to step back the moment Jeffrey is fully seated, but he does, and a few seconds later he hears a soft electrical hum and Jeffrey's whole body goes rigid in the chair. The whining reverberation is like nails on a chalkboard; he puts his hands over his ears and steps farther back.

Jeffrey's face twists with anger. "What's going on?"

He can't move.

Kyle watches, horrified, as he works his way from irritated all the way to pissed off in moments, thrashing as if invisible ropes hold him in place from head to toe.

Kyle stands there for what seems like an eternity before Clara reveals herself in the doorway, armed with chemical spray.

At this point, Jeffrey can't so much as move his jaw to speak. His expression is frozen in rage and his violent thoughts batter Kyle's mental barriers like invisible fists. Several of these punches land, and Kyle is about two seconds away from collapsing under the strain of fending off the blows that follow when Clara puts a hand on his shoulder.

"Any change?" she asks.

"No," he answers, wrapping his arms around himself. He doesn't think he'll ever be able to forget the ugliness inside Jeffrey's head. "Please. I have to—"

She notices how shaken he is. "What did he say to you?"

"He didn't have to *say* anything," he whispers, shoulders hunching inward. He feels weak and hates it. "How is Brian?"

"Stable," she says, the softening of her tone as comforting as a hug. "He's with Erica and Elisa."

Kyle blinks. "At Erica's apartment?"

"No. There's—" Clara pauses, and in this moment he realizes that she is about to reveal something Elisa and Clara have never shared with him. "We have a facility. It's sort of a medical treatment center slash research lab."

"Does Brian know about this?" Kyle asks.

"No," she answers. "At least, not yet. We do a lot of research, as the result of what we learn when we treat vampires and victims of vampire attacks. He's perfect for the group, naturally, but we weren't sure if he could handle it on top of everything else he does."

Kyle shudders. All this unsettles him, and Jeffrey is still here, throwing out the most disgusting mental images. "Is that—is that something you guys invented?" he asks, motioning to the chair. As far as he can tell, some sort of mesh is laid over the chair's surface.

"When we've got time, I'll explain how it works, if you're interested," she says, sounding impatient. "For now, I'm just relieved that it does."

"You—this was the *test drive*?"

"I wasn't supposed to tell you that," she answers dryly. "We'll discuss it later. The police are on their way."

He hesitates, one last time. "What are they going to do to him?"

"I'm reporting him as an intruder, and once he's in the system we'll have him linked to the center break-in," she says.

"He killed people on his way here," Kyle says.

"Well, then. That makes this even easier." She pauses. "What you said back in the park—it's true? He tried to take your blood, and you thought you'd killed him?" He nods.

"If I were you I'd go home, clear up that missing person thing—put it behind you. You should get a fresh start, like we all did." She touches his arm. "And depending on what he says to the cops, you may be called in for questioning later. Better to clean up your paper trail now, before they use it to find you."

He would feel a lot more compelled to thank her for all her help and advice if he could stop sensing Jeffrey, but he can't, and all he wants right now is to go to Brian and forget everything that's happened tonight. Tomorrow they can tackle logistics.

"Can you give me the address?" he asks, and she nods.

*

"Kyle," Erica breathes, surprised.

"Clara—"

She nods. "I figured. Come in. He's okay, but you won't be able to talk to him."

Kyle can tell by how strongly the room reeks of Brian's blood that it was pretty bad. He senses, wafts of scent, layer upon layer of fear: Brian's and Erica's and even John's. Brian had been in *very* bad shape. Kyle steadies himself with a deep breath as she leads him through to the back of the complex.

"It was bad," he says.

"It was bad," she confirms.

She opens a door onto a small room and motions him inside. Brian is a bandage-swathed, blood-streaked lump attached to lines and machines on a hospital bed in the corner of the room. Kyle feels a pain so sharp at the sight, it actually makes his vision go black. He turns away and buries his head against Erica's side. Warm tears spring into his eyes.

"He's stable," she reminds him, her jaw strong and eyes bright. "He's going to be okay. It was mostly blood loss and shock."

"It was just the bite? You're sure?" He can't bring himself to verbalize some of the things he'd seen in Jeffrey's head.

She frowns, then nods. She understands what he's referring to. "It was just the bite."

Kyle shudders. "Thank you. Thank you for—everything, for saving him—"

"He's one of the strongest people I know," she says. "And when he wakes up he's gonna be pissed as hell that I didn't invite him here sooner; so I guess saving his life is good leverage to have." She smiles playfully, obviously trying to get him to smile back.

He feels his lips quirk, but it's not quite a smile. "Can I sit with him?"

She nods. "I'm going to go clean up." She stops at the door and turns to look at him over her shoulder. "I feel responsible for this. I sent him some information that made you look suspicious. It's why he went looking for you, to ask you about it, and then I turned you away later, and—I'm sorry, Kyle, if I had anything to do with this happening. Brian is my best friend, but I should have given you the chance to speak for yourself. I should have realized how much you care about him."

Kyle's heart thuds painfully in his chest. Logically, he knows that Jeffrey would have gotten to him one way or another, and Brian would have been injured or killed in the process no matter when, where or how it played out. But knowing that Brian might have died tonight thinking the worst of him... he doesn't know what to say to her. But now isn't the time to be angry at her, either, and he isn't sure if he even has the right to be angry when none of this would have happened if not for him.

It's not the time to fall all over himself and reassure her of his innocence, either. Right now all he wants to do is sit quietly and feel Brian's pulse against his fingertips. So he gives her a brief nod and she leaves, and for the first time since all of this craziness began Kyle sets his sights on Brian, lying there so broken and small and filthy, and lets himself cry.

The first thing Brian thinks when he wakes up is that Kyle looks like death warmed over, and the second thing is that he wants to feed him, but knows immediately that he can't. Just how he knows this takes longer to sort out.

His eyes wander hazily over the drip in his arm and the equipment beeping around him. It's no hospital he recognizes, but if Kyle is here then it has to be okay.

He'd been hurt. Right. Check. Drained by a vampire of freakish strength and a distinct lack of mental clarity. And then—there had been others. A conversation by water, trees—from there the sequence of events grows fuzzy and unreachable, and trying to follow it exhausts him. He focuses instead on closing his fingers around Kyle's slender, pale forearm, which rests on the bed beside him.

Kyle jerks awake before Brian's fingers complete the journey, his bloodshot eyes snapping open, his stark black pupils huge when they first focus and contracting as he wakes, bleeding blue around the edges.

"Brian," he says, and it comes out so desperately Brian's chest aches.

"Was looking for you," Brian replies. His mouth is as dry as cotton and tastes like blood. He can barely move his tongue.

"Oh, honey," Kyle breathes. "I'm so sorry."

"'M'I okay?"

"You lost a lot of blood but yes, you're okay now." Kyle's eyes shimmer with tears. "This is all my fault."

"Why your fault?" Even as he asks the question, their conversation begins to slip from his mental grasp.

"If I had been honest with you from the start, none of this would've happened," Kyle says miserably.

Brian wants to respond, to ask questions, but he can feel a wave of unconsciousness approaching, and before he can even try to fight it he's sliding under.

Michael arrives that evening and, once he's up to speed, lays into Kyle so harshly that the rest of the group gives them the room. They only stop short of shouting the walls down because the noise they're making wakes Brian.

"This isn't over," Michael says, eyes black and quivering, jabbing a finger at him. "You are responsible for this."

"I love him," Kyle says, shakily. "I know that this is my fault, but I *love* him, and I'm going to do everything in my power to—"

"He wants to see you, Michael," Erica interrupts, sticking her head in the doorway cautiously.

Michael's mask of anger cracks at that, and for one painful moment Kyle can see all of his fear for and love of his brother on his face. He's gone before Kyle can utter another word.

"You okay?" Erica asks.

"Who cares if I'm okay?" Kyle asks. "He's right. I almost got Brian killed, and if it hadn't been for Clara and Elisa and you—I did *nothing*. I can't protect him. I couldn't even protect him from myself."

Erica waits for him to finish, and then takes him to a room that has a water cooler and a refrigerator in it.

"There's blood in the fridge," she says, sitting him down. "Eat. Next door there's a room with a cot. Sleep. You're no good to anyone in this state, Brian least of all." She sighs. "There'll be plenty of time to rake yourself over the coals later. For now we need to stick together. Michael is angry for a good reason, but you also have your own; don't forget that."

Her words feel like the insistent jabbing of fingertips trying to jostle him from an angry stupor, when all he wants to do is continue being upset with himself in peace. He doesn't want to sleep—what if

Brian needs him and he's not there? But it's true that he is exhausted, and he can feel the jagged edges of his self-hatred sharpen, looking for any excuse to continue shredding him, and with Michael here, ready, willing and able to help that along—

Erica is right. He needs to disconnect. So he does as he's told, and falls asleep the moment his head touches the pillow.

✷

All Brian wants is for Kyle to wake up.

Throughout the ordeal of his recovery after Erica finished putting him back together, of dealing with Michael's anger and of trying to convince them to let him leave his hospital bed, all he's been able to think about are those blue eyes opening and looking at him, seeing him, connecting the two of them again.

He's been so completely cut off from everything else that makes his life his life, that he *needs* this. He needs Kyle to be there because nothing else is.

Against everyone's advice, he drags himself out of bed, uses a wheelchair to get to the room where Kyle has been hiding and hauls himself onto the sour-smelling cot where Kyle is passed out. He closes his eyes and wraps his arms and legs around Kyle, letting the warmth of his body seep into his own, and goes to sleep.

He's not sure how long they stay that way, but Erica wakes him several times to check his vitals, change his bandages, clean him as best she can and make him drink something that tastes like vitamins and chocolate-flavored sugar. She removes the drip but gives him some pretty heavy doses of oral painkillers in exchange, drugs that make him fall deeply into vivid, frightening dreams.

In the middle of the night almost a day and a half later, Kyle finally wakes up, goes stiff in Brian's arms and rolls over into his chest, fingers feeling for him in the dark. Neither of them needs visual confirmation to know who the other is, and Brian feels Kyle go limp with relief, the press of his face against his neck and the creep of his fingers down his back.

"Brian," he breathes, sounding miserable but relieved.

The drugs have worn off somewhat and Brian is in pain, but it's nothing compared to what it was just a day ago, and he's determined to remain lucid so Kyle doesn't call for Erica.

"Are you okay?" he asks, smoothing a hand down Kyle's back.

"Your brother hates me."

Brian would laugh, if that wouldn't make the pain worse. "He doesn't hate you. He's—worried." He pauses, unsure if now is the time, and then decides that he can't wait any longer. "Would you please tell me what happened?" His voice is a wreck and he's weak, but he's as clearheaded as he's going to get at the moment, and he needs to know *something* before he slips under again.

"Right—right now? Are you sure you want to—right now?"

"Please."

Kyle draws closer, tucking himself against Brian's chest. "The vampire who broke into the center—his name is Jeffrey Simmons. We went to school together. For most of our lives, actually. Elementary, middle and high school. He lived down the block from my aunt and uncle. He—he was always a weird kid. Quiet and awkward when he was little. Sort of mean when he got older, because he got bigger. But he never really fit in with any crowd, and—sometimes I thought we were friends. I always got this weird vibe from him, though. Never really knew where we stood. One day he'd call me names; the next he'd try to be nice to me. I had no idea he was—like me, in some ways."

"Gay? Or a vampire?"

"Gay," Kyle answers. "I had a feeling that he was, but he wasn't out or in, you know? Every now and then he'd ask me to hang out with him after school. I just thought he was messing with me; a lot of the guys at school did, in that exact way, all the time.

"Anyway, um. After graduation he said he needed to talk to me alone. I had no idea what he wanted to talk about, but I figured we wouldn't be seeing each other much after graduation, so I didn't see the harm in going with him to the band room after we got our diplomas. When we got there he started ranting about how I'd rejected him unfairly, all these years. About how much he cared for me, and why hadn't I ever figured it out? He wanted us to be boyfriends. Didn't I know that we were perfect for each other? The truth is, I had never realized that he felt anything for me. For a minute I thought maybe I had done something wrong, maybe I missed something or led him on? But I hadn't. I know I didn't.

"He started to talk about me, about us, as if we'd had something going for years, as if I were just being cruel, ignoring his feelings and keeping him at a distance. I guess he'd expected me to make a move or something before we graduated? I tried to let him down easily, but he just wasn't listening. Nothing I said seemed to penetrate, you know? It was like he was in his own little world and I was just a toy that was saying the wrong thing every time he pulled my string. He refused to let me leave the room.

"When I tried to force my way out, he—grabbed me. I tried to get away from him, to scream, but he was prepared. He had the spray, and the school was deserted by then." Kyle begins to shake. "So after he paralyzed me and tied me down, he cut me. He cut himself. He took the blood right from my veins. I grew disoriented from the blood loss, but my survival instincts kicked in eventually, and—he wasn't prepared for how strong I could be, even injured, I guess. The spray only works for short periods of time, so you have to keep applying it, and I guess he didn't know that either. I broke the chair he had tied me to, got my arms free and I—attacked him. Viciously.

"I—I was sure that I killed him. There was so much blood, he was so broken and still, and I had no reason to think—so I ran. I ran and a week later I was in Chicago. I've been hiding here ever since. When we spoke in the park after he attacked you the other night, he explained that he'd thought it was his humanity that had kept us from being together. That if we were 'equals', especially if we shared my blood, I'd want him the way that he wanted me."

Brian stares into the darkness, his eyes burning and his heart racing. "God, honey," he breathes, tightening his arms around Kyle.

"I had no idea that he broke into the center, but I suspected. I could have told you, warned you then—but I had no proof, and the authorities didn't find anything. I wanted so badly for it to be a coincidence, to just—forget that it had ever happened. And then, that night—I could feel your fear and pain, and I *knew*—I knew I'd screwed up." Tears fall, warm and slow, soaking Brian's shirt. "I found you. I led him away and let Elisa and Clara take you, hoping that you'd be okay, that I hadn't been too late. Clara had some technology back at the club, some kind of paralyzing net, and I was able to lure Jeffrey into it without having to fight him, and she called the police."

"This is—this is what you've been hiding? That you thought you killed this guy in self-defense?" Brian asks, digging his fingers into Kyle's back.

"Murder is murder," Kyle answers, voice shaking. "If I'd told you what I'd done without knowing that I hadn't actually killed him, you never would have—"

"You don't know that," Brian interrupts. "He hurt you. He could've killed you. How could I judge you for doing whatever you could to survive that?"

It's only then, when Kyle begins to cry, that Brian realizes he's the first person to offer him forgiveness and consolation, and to acknowledge that even though it's not okay, it's *over*; and that he can, at the very least, stop feeling responsible for the taking of a life.

"You almost died," Kyle breathes out shakily, "because of me."

"I almost died because that guy is seriously messed up," Brian replies, tugging Kyle half on top of him; even though it's uncomfortable, he needs to be closer. "Yes, you should have told me sooner. But that doesn't matter now."

All at once, he feels exhausted. He isn't going to be able to stay awake for much longer and he knows that Kyle can feel this, too.

"Please sleep," Kyle whispers. "Please just get better, okay?"

He's already sliding under.

All told, they spend about a week at the facility. Elisa, Clara, Janice, Michael, Erica and John all take turns caring for Brian and keeping both him and Kyle surrounded by friendly faces. In Michael's case the expression is more of a wary glare, but as the days pass and Brian is able to talk to him and explain what happened, his shoulders loosen and his glares morph into a stiff silence.

Kyle doesn't go out of his way to engage Brian's brother. Michael has the story and, if he doesn't want to forgive Kyle, then it is what it is. Hours of conversation with Clara have left Kyle feeling centered, and his vampire nature has allowed him to withdraw from the terrible events. He's calmer, stronger and ready to begin to move on, even if he hasn't been able to forgive himself.

Erica rotates Brian's work schedule so that he can take his vacation and sick time to recover without losing pay or credits, but all he wants is to go home.

"I'm sure my plants are dead," he says.

Kyle smiles. "Your plants are fine. Your mental state, however..."

He knows that Brian is panicking about a lot of things—missing work, falling out of touch with his regulars at the clinic, failing to maintain the professional and educational correspondences that are the lifeblood of his career, and all the things that keep him as busy as a medical student can be. He just can't be happy when he's idle, and Kyle worries that it's affecting his recovery.

By the end of the week he's climbing the walls and unbearable even to Kyle, who begs Erica to give them permission to leave.

"He'll hit his phone and laptop the second I let him out of my sight; his blood pressure will go through the roof," she protests.

"I'll drag him off the electronics as often as I can, I promise. He's stable enough, isn't he?"

"He is," she confirms.

Elisa visits on the day they're finally allowed to leave. She greets Kyle with a crisp, "Let's talk."

Kyle knows: she wants the whole story. She's visited less than Clara in the past week and has never managed to get Kyle on his own; he isn't surprised that she's insisting now, while Brian gets one final checkup before they go home.

It's a difficult conversation, but all she does is nod and tense up here and there.

"That's the full story, *gato*?" she asks, when he goes quiet. "Those are all the surprises I can count on from you?"

"That's it. And I'll be back at work as soon as Brian doesn't need medical supervision, I promise."

She smirks, but there's a softness in her eyes that he's never seen before, and she surprises him even further when she leans over and hugs him. "Make sure he gets back into fighting, ninja-doctor form. There's a place for him here in the lab, if he wants it. But don't tell him just yet. Keep me in the loop."

"Is it for us or them, this place? Really?" Kyle asks, after allowing himself a moment of surprise at her offer. It's a question that's been plaguing him ever since he found out about the facility.

"Both," she says, her eyes darkening. "Times are changing, kid."

Kyle has the feeling that this is where she intends to end the conversation, but the curiosity in his eyes stops her at the door.

"That doesn't mean much considering that I know nothing about this place aside from the fact that you have a lot of cool weapons and a lab that turns Brian's head faster than my tightest pair of jeans," he says, smirking.

She rolls her eyes fondly, crosses her arms and leans back against the door. "What, you think it's that easy? 'Ask and ye shall receive'?"

He knows that she wants to tell him something, or she wouldn't still be standing there waiting for him to continue asking.

"Give me something, Elisa," he says, catching her powerful gaze. "I'm walking out that door today with an injured boyfriend, a whole lot of trauma, and not much else."

She inclines her head, her eyebrows twitching in acknowledgment, and then she holds out her arms. "This is our baby, Clara and I. The club is how it started. Blood coming in, blood going out. We paid attention, kept records. Humans learned to trust us. Vampires learned to trust us. Turns out that science can be fun, educational and profitable." She takes in and lets out a breath. "And then the government found us."

Kyle's heart skips a beat at that. "What happened?"

"This was years before vampires were outed, but there were already signs that it was coming. We saw the writing on the wall, and so did they. We worked out a contract with them at the federal level—our research and expertise in exchange for their funding and the chance to craft policy. The chemical spray that the police use against vampires? Us. The blood clinic feeding program? Us."

"God," he breathes. "All this time...?"

She nods, and the pride on her face bleeds into unease in a way that he's never seen before. "It hasn't been all power lunches and poolside business negotiation, let me tell you." Her shoulders fall, and then rise again determinately. "The longer vampires exist in the public eye, the harder it gets. What worked five years ago doesn't work today. Even our perspective—" She stops, seems to reconsider her choice of words, and then goes on, "Look. It's not only Brian we want to see back here. You're smart. You grew up out there, in a world where vampires and humans exist side by side because they have to, because that's just the way it is. Your experience could be valuable to us. You could make a difference." She tosses her hair back. "It's not always glamorous but it's a big fucking deal, for them and for us."

"You want me to keep working for you?" he asks.

He's equal parts terrified and excited by her offer because, like so much of what they've shared, it's both vague and potentially dangerous. It's also instantly appealing to him.

"You have somewhere else you gotta be?" she asks, smiling spicy-sweet at him, and then she turns, takes the doorknob in hand and looks at him over her shoulder, taking in the enthralled expression on his face. "I'll see you at work."

He isn't sure whether she means the club or this underground facility. When he thinks about it, though, the distinction doesn't seem to matter; he's in, and he's sure that she already knows it.

10

Erica comes bearing her mother's best culinary efforts, and Brian has to admit that he would have been thrilled to see her even if she'd shown up empty-handed. The wound on his neck is giving him trouble and he misses Kyle; being alone after a week of having him there to hold onto has been difficult.

"Sustenance," she chirps.

He steers her into the kitchen before he even says hello.

"You're the best," he says, digging out plates and silverware.

"How's the wound? Need help changing your bandage?"

"No, thanks, I took care of it this morning," he replies, sitting opposite her and serving them both. "It's getting there."

"Heard from Kyle?" she asks as they eat.

"Things are strained with Michael, but they're making progress. He's been a huge help, obviously. They found out who filed the missing person report. It was actually one of the teachers at the school, his drama teacher." Erica nods. Brian chews. "Jeffrey's in the system, but apparently he's gone catatonic. If he names Kyle in the future there may be more questioning, but as of right now there's no paper connection between them." He sighs. "They were able to prove that Jeffrey killed those people, so he's most likely going to disappear anyway."

Erica stares off into space and pushes food around her plate. "Not that he doesn't deserve punishment—but god, sometimes I hate this system."

"It'll change," Brian says, and truly believes it. "We'll change things. Make it better."

She smiles, soft and slow, and says, "Speaking of that..."

*

Just outside the city, Kyle takes the iPod buds out of his ears, turns to Michael and says into the blackness of the car's interior, "I love your brother. I'm not going to stop loving him. I don't like going against your wishes—I really like you, Michael—but it comes down to him and me, and if he still wants me after this I'm not going anywhere."

Michael is quiet for a long time. Seeing Brian in that hospital bed left him shaken, but Kyle isn't going to back down. It's true that he hasn't forgiven himself for what happened, but Brian has, and for now that has to be enough.

"I'm the only family he has," Michael says finally, his voice strained. "Our dad—he doesn't—after Mom died, he started a new life. Brian and I, we were never enough for him—Mom held it all together, and without her—" He sighs. "I don't want to see him get hurt."

"I meant it when I said that everything about me is out in the open now," Kyle says. "And I am truly sorry for what happened. Whether or not you accept that apology is up to you."

They don't talk for a while. The car eats up the miles, inky and endless, the road nearly empty at this time of night.

Michael sighs heavily. "I guess someone has to keep him distracted while I act like an idiot at my wedding," he says, smirking at Kyle through the rearview mirror.

Kyle smiles back, relief flooding his chest. "I do owe you now, I guess."

*

Kyle gets home in the middle of the night, just in time to bring Brian his medication.

"Tell me what happened," Brian says, but the drugs are already making him sleepy.

"Tomorrow," Kyle whispers against the back of his neck, pulling the blankets over them.

Tomorrow brings dry mouth and discomfort and a clumsy shower. Kyle washes him while he keeps his bandage dry (he's been managing by himself, but it's nice not to have to).

They don't even exchange good mornings until ten o'clock, when they curl up in bed again on clean sheets (again, thanks to Kyle), and Kyle feeds him fresh fruit for breakfast, little chunks of ripe melon and banana that go down easily with little to no chewing required.

By now the drugs have worn off, for the most part. Brian feels stronger and clearheaded today, and the sticky-sweet glide of juice between Kyle's fingers and his lips almost escalates into a pleasant make-out session—until Kyle pokes him in the ribs and tells him to breathe because he seems to have forgotten how and has begun to list dangerously to one side.

"You're still out of commission," he admonishes with a smile, his cheeks bright pink from the few kisses they've exchanged.

"I'm going to forget how to have sex at this rate," Brian replies. He drops his hungry gaze to Kyle's mouth. "I miss you feeding from me, too, so much." He traces Kyle's upper lip with a fingertip, fully aware of the placement of the fangs tucked up into his gums.

Kyle's pupils go wide. "Even after what Jeffrey did to you?"

"Not the same thing," Brian replies, cupping Kyle's jaw in his palm, but then he shakes his head. "We should be talking about Mansford, I'm sorry."

Kyle smiles, kissing him. "Since we can't do anything about *that* right now, yes."

"So tell me about Mr. Lyttle."

"He was my drama teacher," Kyle says. "Apparently a scholarship came up around graduation time that he thought I might want to apply for, so he got my aunt and uncle's home number from the school, and when he called them the day after graduation they told him that they had no idea where I was, that I'd never come home from the ceremony. They just assumed that I had gone out partying." Kyle rolls his eyes. "As if that makes any sense; they knew I had no friends. But Mr. Lyttle knew for sure that I had intended to go home after I picked up my diploma. The next morning he found the carnage in the band room and figured there had to be a connection. He told me that he had intended to call my relatives again that afternoon anyway to ask after me, but when he saw the mess he wanted to make sure I was okay."

Brian frowns, tightening his arms around Kyle's waist. "Oh, wow."

"It's weird; I didn't even know he cared," Kyle says, sighing. "I hardly knew what to say. I thanked him and gave him my number and email address."

Brian smiles. "I bet he was happy to see you."

"I wanted to talk to him about Jeffrey, but I couldn't," Kyle says. "Obviously."

"Michael and Erica and I are going to do everything we can to make sure that he gets the same treatment as any other criminal," Brian says, stroking Kyle's shoulder.

"I don't know why I care, I just—there's obviously something seriously wrong with him aside from just violent tendencies. He deserves a fair shot at treatment as much as punishment."

"It's good to care about the rules meaning something," Brian says. "They *should* mean something."

There's a pause, and Kyle continues. "So—then my aunt and uncle showed up. Someone at the station assumed that I wanted them to be notified, because they were listed in the paperwork as my guardians. I don't know what I was supposed to feel, but I told them I was happy and settled and that was that. We didn't talk much or even say goodbye, really; they slipped out while I was with Mr. Lyttle and the detective."

"Geez. Are you okay with that?" Brian asks, surprised that this part of the story comes across as an afterthought.

"I feel like I shouldn't be," he says. His eyes go distant as he stares out the far window. "But I think I am. I never had any real love for them, and I'm pretty sure the feeling was mutual."

"And Michael?" he asks.

"We bickered a lot. And then he went into professional lawyer mode with Mr. Lyttle and the police. I think that's why they asked so few questions; he scared the crap out of them." Brian chuckles at this. "On the way home he was quiet, which made me nervous because I don't think I've ever seen your brother quiet. We had it out in the car, sort of, and I—I just told him that I wasn't going to give up on fixing things." He presses his face into Brian's neck. "I told him that I wasn't going to stop loving you."

The urge to tell him that he doesn't *have* to fix things—or that at the very least, if there is something to fix, they'll fix it together—is so prominent in Brian's mind; but he knows how important it is for Kyle to work through his feelings, so he stifles that urge.

"I'm glad," he says. "I know how much it was upsetting you to fight with him."

"I deserved it," Kyle replies. "But I'm dating you, not your brother. He has to understand that."

Brian grins. "I saw those looks the first night you two met. You thought he was hot."

"Observation of good genetics does not equal attraction, sir."

"That was pretty smooth."

"I thought so."

Brian laughs, trying to ignore the throb at his neck. "Plans for today?"

"I need to get back to work," Kyle answers, "if I expect to afford school supplies this semester. I emailed the admissions office about changing my paperwork to reflect my real name—told them a whole long family sob story—and they said that I could start classes while the change goes through." He grins. "When they saw that I paid my tuition bill in cash and up front, they were suddenly very willing to work with me."

"Let me know if you need any help," Brian says.

"I may need help surviving Elisa's wrath. She's probably come up with at least a dozen new insults for me since the last time we spoke."

Brian laughs. "I won't lie; she's tried a few of them on me already."

"Oh, god," Kyle groans. "I am not surprised." He smiles. "Did they talk to you about...?"

Brian nods, smiling back. "Yeah. I've got a lot to think about, but it's—I don't think I could say no, you know?"

"I'm so excited for you," Kyle says, lacing their fingers. "It's what you've always wanted: you can do research *and* work with patients. And one day, your own practice."

"I want all of that so badly," Brian replies, his mind spinning with the possibilities. "I just have to teach myself how to slow down and not try to do it all in one day."

"I could provide distraction at key moments," Kyle replies, scratching a fingernail down Brian's chest with a coy little smile.

"Is this a key moment, do you think?" he asks, licking his bottom lip.

"Let's find out," Kyle answers, straddling his waist.

It's weeks before feeding comes up again, mostly because Kyle refuses to broach the topic. He wants Brian to recover, physically and mentally, from what Jeffrey put him through. He doesn't understand why Brian would want fangs anywhere near him after what happened. Brian protests that Jeffrey didn't bite the side of his neck that Kyle always bites, and continues to insist that the two acts aren't even in the same book, much less on the same page.

Kyle isn't convinced, but something is definitely missing from their relationship without it. The intimacy it results in. The satisfaction it creates in Kyle to take what he needs from the person he loves who is more than eager to give it to him. Most importantly, he realizes that it's about Brian wanting to take care of him.

They celebrate Kyle's first week of classes with a ludicrously expensive dinner out, and spend the rest of the evening in bed.

Now Kyle is on top of Brian, softening inside him as he licks tracks of sweat from the sharp curve of his collarbone.

Brian could say any number of things to shatter Kyle's resolve—he's had his mouth buried against Brian's tender neck for a while now—but it's the direct approach that finally does it, in the end.

He stares up at Kyle, his cheeks still flushed with arousal, eyes wide and wet, pulse fluttering visibly at his throat when he breathes out, "Drink?"

"Brian," Kyle begins, worry crowding his chest.

Brian kisses him, licks into his mouth and along his gumline, where his fangs hide, one lapse of control away from coming down, as always. Kyle shivers, feeling the touch everywhere. He's been feeding from customers at work, so this isn't about need. It's about desire. He wants Brian's blood the same way that he wants Brian; with an uncontrollable hunger made up of equal parts love and lust.

"It's been so long," Brian replies, fingers trailing over Kyle's sweaty back in tentative sweeps. "Please?" His voice goes rough and low. "Miss it, miss the way it feels when we're connected like that."

Kyle swallows thickly, taken over by the temptation. He stiffens again inside Brian simply at the thought, unable to control his response to this teasing, and he knows that Brian can feel it, that Brian knows how close he is to giving in.

"Do you feel me in your head when I feed from you?" he asks, hips jolting.

"Oh," Brian moans, moving underneath him. "Oh, baby, yes, I— don't stop."

"It doesn't freak you out?" he asks, shivering when Brian's body contracts around the base of his cock. He only came maybe ten minutes ago, and they're both still so sensitive—it feels amazing to be inside Brian, hardening again, without having pulled out between rounds.

Brian rolls his pelvis, his belly hitching with uneven breaths. "*Kyle*—please—n-no, it doesn't. I love it. Feel close to you, feel so *loved* by you."

Kyle can't help it; his hips are already moving and Brian's ass is fluttering around him, smooth from friction and stretching. He presses his face into the dip of Brian's throat and just breathes him in: human smell, male musk and simple human desire. Though he doubts that Brian can feel him in return just yet, he can feel Brian with his mind, his thoughts crowded with sharp-edged longing. Brian isn't exaggerating; he truly wants what he's asking for, and Kyle can't deny him any longer.

Kyle's belly swoops and his heart stutters and everything goes white around the edges of his vision. His head swims and grows dizzy with anticipation; he can taste and feel Brian's skin against his lips, so soft, so fragile, so easily *hurt*, and the power in him rings out like a symphony. He wants it, so badly, and Brian is going to let him have it, and that never loses its element of heady surprise.

Brian squirms and his fingernails scrabble down Kyle's back. "Please—please—"

An electric jolt shoots down Kyle's spine as his fangs slip down. He breathes shakily, sliding his fingers along Brian's arms, pushing them over his head and down against the pillows. He laces their fingers together there as he bites down, hard and fast. Brian's body goes rigid with the pain and he cries out, but the moment Kyle pulls his teeth out he goes as limp as a kitten, his eyes rolled back and his body clenched around Kyle's cock.

"Yes," he hisses, forearms flexing against Kyle's hold. "Just like that. Take it, honey."

It all goes fuzzy when Kyle starts swallowing the blood that spurts between his lips. It's never as messy as the movies make it out to be, but he still has to be careful not to let any escape his mouth as he pulls, swallow after swallow going thin and warm and salty down his throat. When he breaks away, the blood is already congealing, but not enough to prevent it from trickling just a little in small streaks of dark red, black and brown, and sluggishly rolling across Brian's beautiful brown skin.

"Gorgeous," he groans, licking at the blood. "So gorgeous."

"Let me ride you," Brian whimpers, looking hazy but determined.

Kyle releases his hold on Brian's forearms, intending to use his strength to roll them over so that Brian doesn't have to make the effort; but Brian is already climbing on top of him without letting him slide out. He cries out when he sits down, taking Kyle to the root again.

The blood trickle trips down and over his collarbone. Kyle sits up to lick at the sticky remains while Brian cradles his head against his chest and rocks down into his lap. Kyle slides his mouth around the blood-sticky nipple and it goes hard between his lips. He puts one hand on Brian's ass and drags him in closer, pushing deeper inside of him.

"Feel so good," Brian whimpers, sinking his fingers into Kyle's hair as he fucks down around his cock. "Come in me. Want to feel you come in me."

Kyle whines, shifting his sticky mouth to Brian's, where it receives a thorough licking before Brian latches on, bouncing in his lap. The friction is perfect and he fulfills Brian's wish not long after, holding him by his thick hips and pounding up into him. Brian remained soft through round two, and so Kyle finds nothing to amuse himself with after he comes; but that's common for them. He kisses Brian and rolls them onto their sides, sliding out with a grunt.

Brian blushes at the messy result, cheeks rosy under Kyle's fingertips.

"Mm, let me," Kyle says, reaching down and sweeping his fingers through the mess, then dipping inside to push out what remains—cheekily taking his time—before reaching around with a tissue to dab off the worst of it.

"You like that a little too much," Brian teases.

Kyle uses a second tissue, wet from a bottle of water on the night-stand, to swipe at the blood that's tracked all over Brian's neck and chest. "I would be offended, but you're not making the judging-you face, so..."

"That would require the use of all of my facial muscles. So, not happening right now."

"I didn't think so," Kyle replies, laughing. Sleepy contentment settles over them. It feels good to be so close, to be so *sure* of another person, especially after what they've been through. But there's something else. He can feel it. He tilts his head at Brian. "You're thinking."

"I've exceeded my sarcasm quota for the afternoon so I'll just say: Yep, I am."

"What about?"

He stares at Kyle for a long moment, blinking more slowly than usual. He's spacey from the blood loss. Kyle doesn't want a serious conversation if he's wiped out, but he doesn't seem to be that far gone. He holds his breath, exhales, and then asks, "Would you consider moving in with me? Or—even better—getting a new place together?"

Oh.

Kyle isn't sure why, but what flashes through his mind now is the first time he saw Brian, looking so handsome in his scrubs, behind a window of reinforced glass at the blood clinic. The memory is hazy with the hunger and desperation of that moment, but he can still clearly recall how caring that face had been; Brian had been the first person to show him kindness since he'd fled Mansford. He recalls feeling safe, for just a moment. Despite the fact that they were perfect strangers, he had felt then as if he'd found someone he could trust.

He recalls the flirtatious conversations that followed, and the making out, and the silly dates they'd gone on in those first few weeks. He recalls everything he hadn't said, how he'd wanted to protect them both from his past, and thinks about how much he regrets that decision now. He recalls being forgiven.

He kisses Brian, his heart pounding. "I'd love that," he says, pulling back to stare into Brian's eyes. "I—yes. Yes."

"Let's start looking today," Brian replies, grabbing his hands. "Let's start right now, come on, get dressed!" He moves to sit up but wobbles instead, and Kyle puts an arm around him, effortlessly holding him up.

"After you recover a little," he says, grinning. "We have the rest of our lives to worry about interior design choices."

Brian goes still, and stares at him with a loving smile. "Our whole lives, huh?"

There's no taking it back, and he has no desire to. "Don't you think so?"

Brian leans in to press their foreheads together. "I do, yeah. I do."

ACKNOWLEDGMENTS

First and foremost, I'd like to thank everyone at Interlude Press, specifically: Candy, for the once in a lifetime opportunity; Annie, for shrewd editorial advice and a friendly ear; and Lex, for saving me from various technological pitfalls at all hours of the day and night.

Thank you to my parents and my sister, who never encouraged me to do anything but what I felt most passionate about.

Thank you to my husband, Brad, without whom "vampire erotica" may never have been on my list of interests. Your support has made this possible. I love you very much.

Thank you to Erika and Donna, who have always been there, especially in the last year or two, not so subtly reminding me, "Hey, don't people sometimes publish this stuff and get rich and famous?" (I don't know about rich and famous, guys, but it turns out that you were right about the publishing part!)

Thank you to Johnna, who has been my best friend, my cheerleader and my "moose" throughout this entire process. You keep me sane and grounded and inspired, and I am more grateful than I can articulate for every moment that we share.

Thank you to Mandy, who led me by the nose when I said "it's just too PG for me." You consistently prove to know me better than I know myself.

A Reader's Guide to *Bleeding Heart*

Questions for Discussion

1. Contrast the government-run clinics and the blood clubs. Are their purposes in any way similar? How do the blood clubs appeal to the true nature of vampires, and how or why might the government clinics tamper with that?

2. Is there more to the government clinics than simply providing safe sustenance for the vampire population?

3. How do the government clinics serve to control the vampire population? Is this a sign that vampires are integrated into society in the world of *Bleeding Heart*, or that they never will be?

4. If the intent of the government clinics is to homogenize the vampire culture, or eliminate the pleasure component of vampire feeding, what does the government accomplish by this?

5. Kyle and Brian attempt to establish a "normal" relationship based in vampire culture. In a world like the one depicted in *Bleeding Heart*, would that be possible, and what obstacles would they face trying to establish a human/vampire relationship?

6. Biting is the pinnacle of desire for both Brian and for Kyle, a moment when they let go of their restraint. How does this differ from the Kyle's bite work in the blood club? Is there a difference?

7. Through much of *Bleeding Heart,* Kyle keeps part of his past secret out of a sense of shame and a fear of his own nature. How does Kyle's behavior mirror the experience of people who identify as gay.

8. In the world of *Bleeding Heart*, society has acknowledged the existence of vampires, and to a degree allowed them to integrate into human culture. There are signs of continued fear of vampires,

however. What are some examples of this, and how does it influence the power dynamic between Kyle and Brian, both in public and private?

9. At the end of *Bleeding Heart*, it is clear that there is more to the blood club than meets the eye. Is it somehow connected with the government clinics, or is it something else entirely?

Coming in 2015
The *Bleeding Heart* saga continues

Hired by Elisa and Clara to work for the agency that has been guiding vampire-human relations, Brian and Kyle struggle to balance the demands of their work at the secretive underground facility with the needs of their evolving relationship. As they adapt to the demanding pace of their new lives, a security breach puts everyone they know and everything they have been working for in danger.

www.ingramcontent.com/pod-product-compliance
Lightning Source LLC
LaVergne TN
LVHW010100110826
845155LV00028B/418

* 9 7 8 1 9 4 1 5 3 0 0 1 6 *